UNDER LOCKER AND KEY

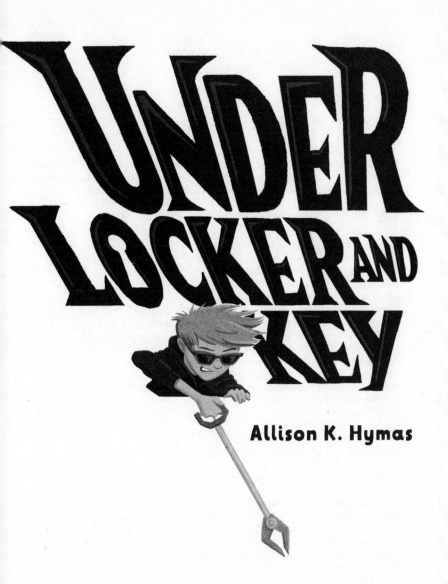

Under Locker and Key

Allison K. Hymas

ALADDIN

NEW YORK   LONDON   TORONTO   SYDNEY   NEW DELHI

ALADDIN

An imprint of Simon & Schuster Children's Publishing Division

1230 Avenue of the Americas, New York, New York 10020

First Aladdin hardcover edition April 2017

Text copyright © 2017 by Allison K. Hymas

Jacket illustration copyright © 2017 by Matt David

Also available in an Aladdin MAX paperback edition.

All rights reserved, including the right of reproduction in whole or in part in any form.

ALADDIN and related logo are registered trademarks of Simon & Schuster, Inc.

For information about special discounts for bulk purchases, please contact Simon & Schuster Special Sales at 1-866-506-1949 or business@simonandschuster.com.

The Simon & Schuster Speakers Bureau can bring authors to your live event. For more information or to book an event contact the Simon & Schuster Speakers Bureau at 1-866-248-3049 or visit our website at www.simonspeakers.com.

Jacket designed by Karin Paprocki

Interior designed by Mike Rosamilia

The text of this book was set in Adobe Caslon Pro.

Manufactured in the United States of America 0317 FFG

10 9 8 7 6 5 4 3 2 1

Library of Congress Cataloging-in-Publication Data

Names: Hymas, Allison K.

Title: Under locker and key / by Allison K. Hymas.

Description: New York : Aladdin, [2017] | Series: MAX |

Summary: "Eleven-year-old Jeremy Wilderson teams up with his rival crime fighter to stop the stealing spree that's wreaking havoc on Scottsville Middle School"—Provided by publisher.

Identifiers: LCCN 2016049810 (print) | LCCN 2016054720 (eBook) |

ISBN 9781481463430 (hc) | ISBN 9781481463423 (paperback) |

ISBN 9781481463447 (eBook)

Subjects: | CYAC: Middle schools—Fiction. | Schools—Fiction. |

Stealing—Fiction. | Mystery and detective stories. |

BISAC: JUVENILE FICTION / Action & Adventure / General. |

JUVENILE FICTION / Social Issues / Friendship.

Classification: LCC PZ7.1.H94 Un 2017 (print) |

LCC PZ7.1.H94 (eBook) | DDC [Fic]—dc23

LC record available at https://lccn.loc.gov/2016049810

Dedicated to Karen Sedar:

For all the time you spent watching over the child I was

and the writer I became,

this one's for you

FIRST OFF, I AM NOT A THIEF.

I am a retrieval specialist. Big difference. Thieves take what doesn't belong to them. They *steal*. Me, I take back the things thieves steal and return them to their rightful owners. The job runs everywhere from crazy to boring to dangerous, but someone has to do it. Kids need protection from the jungle out there.

If you've ever been in middle school, you know what I mean. Bigger kids rip sixth graders off for lunch money, new shoes, whatever. Even teachers contribute to the problem by confiscating cell phones and iPods. I have the highest respect for teachers—my mom is one—but they don't always understand that the cell phone belongs to your dad, not you, and that if you don't give it back right after school, you're grounded.

So I step in. One meeting with me over a cafeteria

lunch or before class and I guarantee to return your stolen property before the late bus leaves. No payment needed—I just ask that you pass my name on to someone else who needs me. And don't tell the teachers that I retrieved your stuff. Or Becca Mills. Especially Becca Mills.

Still convinced I'm a thief? Read on. After you become more familiar with my method, you'll change your mind. Where to begin? How about somewhere exciting . . . ?

The tiles froze my bare knees as I knelt in front of the backpack. I'd like to tell you my heart raced and sweat dripped down my forehead, but I never get nervous on a job that routine. If anything, I felt annoyed at the school for pumping the boys' locker room full of icy air. Why can I almost see my breath in the one room in school where people strip down?

Anyway, the bag didn't belong to me. But the Hello Kitty wallet shoved at the bottom sure didn't belong to the owner of the tough-looking blue-and-black backpack with the X Games key chain.

The client: Carrie Bethesda. First-chair trumpet in the concert band. Sixth grader with a habit of carrying multiple twenties in her wallet. Her parents trusted her with a month of lunch money at a time—a bad idea, as it turned out.

The mark: Adam Lowd. Nothing out of the ordinary: eighth grader with a taste for after-school pizza that left him constantly short on cash. He'd lifted Carrie's wallet during a scuffle in the lunch line, or so Carrie suspected.

She was right. I found the wallet crammed between Lowd's history textbook and a wad of old vocabulary tests. A quick check verified that all $43.75 was still there. This girl was loaded. All that cash might have tempted a real thief to pocket it and leave the client destitute, but I tucked the wallet, bills and all, into the pocket of my hoodie for temporary safekeeping.

My watch beeped. Ten minutes until the end of eighth-grade gym; the students would come back at any minute to change out of their uniforms. Gotta love gym— the only class where you have to leave all your belongings in a room with minimal security. No one's around while class is in session, and half the time, people forget to lock their lockers. On top of that, the gym lockers are so small that backpacks have to be left in the open, like Adam's was. It's like the school *tries* to make my job easier. I zipped Adam's backpack and then left, one hand in my hoodie pocket, resting on the retrieved wallet.

And because it's written in the fabric of the universe that no job can go off without a hitch, with the whir and click of a camera Becca Mills stepped in front of me in the hall outside the gym. "Jeremy Wilderson," she said, twirling her little silver camera by its strap. How did such a tiny girl manage to block the whole hallway?

"Hi, Becca. Shouldn't you be in class?"

"Shouldn't you?"

"Ms. Campbell let us go early after we promised we wouldn't get into mischief." A true statement. That camera wouldn't give her anything on me.

Becca smiled like I imagine a cobra would, if it had lips. "Breaking promises now?"

I raised my hands. "Hey, I'm clean. No trouble here. Why don't you go investigate Scottsville's illegal gum trade? I swear there was some under-the-desk dealing during homeroom."

The twelve-year-old detective stepped closer. Her dark hair gleamed in the June sun coming through the dirty windows. "If there's any illegal gum trading, I bet you're jaw-deep in it."

"After your last three investigations, I'd think you'd know gum trading is not my game."

"Right. Thieving is." Becca's lip curled. "You disgust me."

"Disgusting? Me? I'm a picture of cleanliness, both physically and morally."

"If you're so 'clean,' where is your backpack? Why

were you in the gym locker room right now when your last class of the day is science?"

I sighed. I should have remembered: She'd memorized my schedule back when a history teacher's test answers disappeared between fourth and fifth period, and Becca was certain I'd stolen them. It wasn't me; the teacher remembered he'd left the answers in his car. The way Becca acted, though, you would have thought my innocence personally offended her.

"Like I said, I got out of class early," I said. "It's a nice day. I thought I would put my stuff in my gym locker before I go outside so I wouldn't have to carry it around until after track practice."

Becca's gray eyes narrowed. Her hands lifted, reaching toward the slight bulge in my hoodie pocket. An actual frisking? Really?

"Whoa," I said, backing away. "I know I have an athlete's body, but hands off the abs. People will talk."

Becca drew away. "You *disgust* me."

"You already said that." I shoved my hands into my hoodie's large front pocket. "Now, if you'll excuse me, the sunshine calls."

As I walked away, Becca said, "Your thieving will catch up with you, Wilderson. I'll make sure of it, even if no one else does."

I turned and saluted her, which, judging by her scowl, she did not appreciate.

The bell rang, and I hurried away down halls beginning to crowd with kids. I had to steer through the mess like a getaway driver at rush hour to get back to my locker and retrieve my own backpack. Yeah, I lied to Becca. I wouldn't have to if she would loosen up and see that I provide a necessary service, instead of trying to put me in detention for the rest of my middle school life.

Carrie was waiting outside the instrument room, fussing with her ponytail, biting her lip, and actually *pacing*. I shook my head. I had told her to go about her classes like normal, and she had to act like she stole the principal's car keys (much easier than it sounds, by the way). What if Becca or Adam saw her like this? I beckoned her to follow me into the instrument room.

The loud, busy instrument room makes a great place for handoffs. I use it a lot—band kids need my services more than most people. Instruments have so many loose parts, like reeds and slides and buttons, which have a knack for disappearing just before the winter or spring concert. In return for my help finding mouthpieces that cost way more than a month's allowance, the band kids grant me a certain amount of discretion when I show up in their room. No one bothered me as I leaned into a corner and brought Carrie's wallet out of my pocket.

"You got it!" Carrie said. Or at least I think that's what she said; some trombone player took that moment to run a scale.

"It *was* Adam. He had it in his backpack. You should stop carrying all that money," I said. "Leave some at home in your sock drawer."

Carrie smiled. "I'll do that. I owe you one."

"If you hear of someone who needs something retrieved, send them my way," I said. "But if you feel the need to pay me with something a little more . . . physical, I like chocolate cake. You know where to find me at lunch."

Before I could move, Carrie hugged me. When she let go, I spun on my heel and walked away. It happens a lot. A guy like me—athlete, hero—girls can't resist.

OKAY, FINE. SOME GIRLS *ARE*

immune to my charms, and one of them spent the whole track-and-field practice glaring at me.

This is as good a place as any to tell you more about Becca Mills. I already mentioned she's a detective. To you that probably means she plays with magnifying glasses and watches Sherlock Holmes movies on Saturdays. No. The girl is no amateur.

Becca Mills is the second-smallest girl in the sixth grade and yet throws the shot put for the track-and-field team. The *shot put*. That alone should clue you in to how intimidating she can be. And determined. She'll take cases from private citizens, but she spends most of her time working to eliminate corruption in school. So far she has used her first year of middle school to uncover a cheating-through-text-message organization in the seventh grade, stop a counterfeit-hall-pass scam, and reveal the actual recipe for mystery meat (please, if you have any respect for my sanity, don't make me remember the ingredients). I list only her most impressive cases.

It doesn't help that she's the teachers' darling. She's one of the school's peer mediators; they're students who talk to other students who are having a hard time, but they also look for and rehabilitate the troublemakers. Becca, however, is really good at finding and stopping trouble, so the teachers listen to her when she rats to them. They even give her some leeway with rules, letting her leave class early and such, so she can stop trouble.

Not that *she'd* ever break the rules. That girl hates rule-breakers with an unnatural passion. She knows that I break the rules to help people, but all she cares about is the means, not the end. Becca has made it her personal mission to bring me down because, according to her, if I'm sneaking around, lying, and taking objects from places that are supposed to be secure, I'm a criminal. Apparently, breaking the rules is a *bad* thing even when the rules let people get hurt. Go figure.

It may not have helped that in October I asked her if she liked the idea of joining me in a two-person retrieval team. When I proposed the idea, she looked at me like I was egg salad someone left in a locker over summer break, said she'd rather *eat* said rotten egg salad than spend another minute with a criminal like me, and pushed me against a wall. Next thing I knew, she signed up for peer-mentor detention duty on days she doesn't have track practice just so she'd be there to sneer at me the day she caught me. Which will be never, by the way.

She can't prove anything, and without proof, even her beloved teachers can't do much. The wallet job was nothing new; after every job Becca seems to be right around the corner, waiting for me. Waiting for proof that is never going to come.

Anyway, after doing about fifty sprints at track practice, I went to my backpack where I'd left it by the bleachers near the track only to find that someone had searched it. Oh, Becca had been careful about it, like she always is, but I myself have some expertise in bag searching and know what to look for. My pile of homework papers resembled a sandwich more than a barn that lost a battle with a tornado (like it usually did), and the tongues on my school shoes had been pulled toward the toes. Good thing I'd already handed the wallet off to Carrie; if I'd still had it, *someone* might have gotten the wrong idea about me.

Mom drove me home. She's a language arts teacher for seventh grade and tends to stay late to grade papers, which is why she was around after my practice ended.

"Hey, honey, how was track?" she said when I climbed into the car.

"Pretty good. I'm getting faster."

"I'm glad to hear it."

We spent the rest of the ride with her talking about her job and me staying silent about mine.

My brother, Rick, hogging the TV and being a general pain in my butt, had his legs sprawled all over the couch when I got home. I stood over his head, blocking his view. "Move."

He smiled at me. Nacho cheese spattered the collar of his varsity football T-shirt. "Dr. Evil. I should have known it was you."

"Come on, Rick. I've had a long practice—"

"So have I." Rick's one of the high school football team's quarterbacks. Second string. But he still thinks that gives him special privileges at home.

"—and I really want to chill," I finished.

Rick bent a knee, making six inches of bare couch space. When I didn't move, he smirked. "What is it? Did someone foil one of your dastardly plots?"

Rick knows nothing about my retrieving business. Thought I'd throw that in there. He's just a jerk who found Dad's old spy movies (next to the classic mysteries) and watched them way too many times.

"Maybe," I answered. "I'd love to explain it to you, but you'd have to have a functional brain to understand the details. Sorry."

Mom chose that moment to poke her head in the room. "Jeremy!"

"It's cool, Mom. He doesn't bother me," Rick said. He stood, all six feet two inches of him rising in a mountain of seventeen-year-old meathead. "Maybe someday, though, after you've grown a couple feet," he added after Mom left.

If Becca's the second-smallest girl, I'm the first-smallest boy. My lack of height gives me an edge sprinting and retrieving, but talking to Rick makes me wish I would hit a growth spurt already. And then I'll hit *him*.

Rick was just about to leave the room when someone knocked at the door. The back door.

"I got it!" I raced through the kitchen.

"Suit yourself," Rick said. The couch squeaked as he lay back down.

Only *my* friends/clients come to the back door. One of the necessary precautions when the girl who lives across the street is a private investigator.

I know, right? Becca and her camera even have the prime stakeout spot on my house.

Standing on my back porch was a tall African-American kid wearing a Pittsburgh Steelers jersey and

Philadelphia Eagles fingerless gloves. He wears the gloves September through June because he's afraid of his hands freezing and losing their dexterity. How do I know? I eat lunch with the guy.

"Case," I said, smiling.

He smiled back. "Hey, J."

"What's up? Where's Hack?"

"At home."

"Grounded?"

"Grounded."

I shook my head. "What was it this time?"

"It's hard to catch everything when you're hiding in a closet, but I think Hack broke into his mom's e-mail account and sent a message to the school claiming he had sloth flu." Case choked on a laugh. "Again."

"When's he going to learn that it's not a real thing? How'd you get out?"

"Waited until his mom left and snuck out the back door." Case pulled a pencil out of his back pocket and wove it between his fingers. "Cut short our game of Madden, though. I ended up having to help my sisters with their math homework."

I leaned against the doorframe. "Both of them? Ouch. Any thoughts on getting Hack out of trouble early? I'm favoring plan B on this one."

"No go. Hack's mom caught on, and now she's suspicious whenever she sees Silly String. No, the best bet is plan A."

Plan A stands for "Acting Angelic." Plan B stands for "Busy" and means harassing Hack's mom with anonymous mischief until she's too flustered to enforce Hack's punishment. Nothing major, just a few pranks here and there to keep her busy while Hack spends time with us.

But Case was right: We'd overdone plan B, and Hack acting angelic until his mom lifted his sentence was our best bet. "We'd better hope it works quickly," I said. "What's Hack's record for good behavior?"

"A week. And we had to slip him comic books at school to keep him docile."

"I think I have some back issues of *X-Men*. So, are you here because you want the rest of your video game fix? Or is melting your brain in front of the TV more your style tonight? Although we'd have to budge the Rock first."

Case shifted his weight. "Actually, I need your light fingers."

I eyed him. "Why? You're not that bad at lifting."

"Small things that aren't nailed down, maybe. Besides, I'd rather keep my fingers safe for *my* area of expertise. One callus can be the difference between a flawless stroke of ink and a smudge."

If you were wondering, Case is a forger. Reports, art, doctors' notes . . . It's a good thing he doesn't use his powers for evil.

"I don't think anyone but you would notice. But okay, I'll help. Will this take long?"

Case stuck the pencil above his ear. "It shouldn't take longer than an hour."

"Give me a sec," I said, and then ducked into the house to tell my mom I was hanging out with Case. She told me to have fun; she likes Case. Hack, on the other hand, she doesn't approve of. It may have something to do with his addiction to accessing password-protected computer programs that don't belong to him. And, of course, getting caught.

"So, what did you lose?" I asked as Case and I cut through my neighbors' backyards.

"Well . . . the job's not for me."

I stopped. "It's for a girl, isn't it?"

"No . . ."

"What's her name?"

"You don't know her. She goes to Burdick Charter."

"So it *is* a girl. How'd you meet her?"

"She hired me a few months ago to re-create a couple of doctor's notes for her, just to get her out of gym during the baseball unit. She doesn't like things flying at her at high speeds. Now she has a new project for me."

"Huh." I grinned, but started walking again. "Think you've got a chance if I find whatever she lost?"

"It's not like that."

"Sure. What's the job?"

"Stolen homework. She had to write a five-page report on *Where the Red Fern Grows*, and gave it to a classmate to read over. Today when she asked for it back, the classmate claimed she lost it. Ab—the *client* doesn't believe that. She thinks her friend took the essay to turn in as her own."

"Ouch. Not much of a friend."

Case nodded. "I know. If it doesn't find its way back, the client will have to do it over. And it can't sound too much like the stolen one."

"Double ouch. That book was a real joy to read." We stopped at a well-lit house several streets away from my home. "This it?"

"Yep," Case said, rocking on his heels. "I've already cased it. I know everything about this place now."

"Are you going to tell me where the report is, or am I going to have to dazzle you with my amazing skills?" I asked. "With no preparation, I might add?"

Case grinned. "Come on, *retrieval specialist*. Earn your reputation."

I looked over the house. Neat, orderly. The lawn trimmed to a uniform three inches. Garbage cans lining the street. "The people here are very organized. They'd notice something out of the ordinary. Kid comes home with a stolen report, she doesn't want her mom to see it. Not yet. She'll want to appear to slave over it for a while—when is the assignment due?"

"Tomorrow." Case folded his arms.

"Okay, then, the mark would have told her parents that she'd finished it already. No need to flash it around much, and if she did, she'd want to make sure the essay is ready to take to school." I smirked. "No good stealing homework if you forget to bring it the day it's due. That puts the essay in the backpack. And the backpack is . . ."

I examined the house, which, though it was hard to discern the layout from the sidewalk, looked similar in structure to Hack's house. A window peeked in on the kitchen, where six figures sat at a table. At six o'clock. It looked like this family liked their dinners a bit earlier than the Wilderson and Kingston households did. Made it easy for me, though. All the family members where I could see them.

Behind the family a short hall led into the garage through a mudroom. "Do they drive their kids to school?"

"Don't know. They drive them home," Case offered.

"Then it's there." I pointed at the garage. "In the mudroom. If I was a thief determined to remember to bring the essay, I'd put the backpack near my shoes, on the way out. Her parents probably tell her to put her things there so she won't forget them."

Case clapped a few times. "You are a genius. Now, genius, go and get it."

"I think sarcastically using 'genius' twice in the same breath qualifies as overkill," I said. "You do realize you're asking me to go inside a house I've never been in, where a family is eating dinner, and retrieve the essay without anyone noticing?"

"That's exactly what I'm asking."

I grinned. "Perfect." A job where something could easily go wrong. I'd been hoping for a little excitement.

"What's your first move?"

"I need to get my pathways open. Get out of sight."

Case shrugged and wandered away, around the corner and out of sight, as I hurried to the house.

By the garage door I knelt and took a homemade lockpick set from my pocket. I highly recommend making one of your own, though I have to warn you: If an adult finds out you have one, you could get into trouble. I keep mine in an old wallet, and it has served me well; as fun as crawling through a dusty unlatched window into who knows what selection of pointy lawn tools is, the simple approach often works the best and is a lot safer.

Speaking of the simple approach, sometimes you can go even simpler. I wedged my fingers under the garage door and pulled up. A deep breath and a hoist and the door was up, no lock-picking required. It amazes me how often people leave their houses vulnerable. Do they think I won't just try the door?

I tucked my lockpick set away and waited a moment, but no sound from the house. No one had noticed, or if they had, they didn't comprehend what the squeak and rattle meant. I was good to go.

Smiling, I walked back to the curb, where the family's full garbage cans sat, waiting for the next morning's pickup. I braced myself, kicked one over, then ran for cover beside the house, laughing like a madman.

Like I told Case, on a street like this, anything abnormal gets noticed. I watched as six people emerged from the front door, riled by my act of petty vandalism. It gave them something to look at while I snuck in, unnoticed.

As the parents tried to spot the trash-tipping maniac and right their toppled can, and while other houses opened their doors and yelled questions, I slipped into the garage.

On to the dangerous part. If I had miscounted and

someone had stayed behind in the kitchen, I'd be easily caught. Also, the mark could have moved her backpack to her room, or she could have sisters with similar backpacks, or the essay could have been moved out of the backpack to show to parents. Going in so blind is risky; I could see myself having to creep through a full kitchen, sneak upstairs, find the essay, and make a hasty escape through a second-story window.

What an awesome story that would make later! Man, I love my job.

But as soon as I opened the door from the garage to the mudroom, I felt a little disappointed. The door to the kitchen was shut. In the dim light I saw a backpack on the washing machine, beside the coatrack. Pink and green: a girl's bag. I didn't even have to unzip it; it was already open. No loose papers inside, but two folders and a notebook.

"I'm going to see what's taking them so long." A girl's voice from the kitchen.

Grabbing the folders and the notebook, I slid behind the longest coat on the rack.

The door opened. A girl walked in, opened the door to the garage, and walked out. She didn't even look in my direction.

I opened the first folder, and there it was: a five-page essay on *Where the Red Fern Grows*. In the time it takes for a rumor that the school has banned sodas to scare the whole sixth grade, I had the essay and escaped back into the garage. I crouched behind a car and watched the girl talk to her parents, and they all went back inside through the front door. No one questioned why the garage door was open; the parents, distracted as they were by the hooligan who had knocked over their trash can, were too angry to care.

A simple grab-and-go because people only see what they want to. All I had to do was leave and close the garage door on my way out. This wasn't my first cakewalk, and an amateur mistake like leaving a door or window open could cost me more than I could pay.

I found Case around the corner and tossed him the pages. "Here."

"Be careful with those!" Case caught them and looked them over. "This is exactly her writing style. I'll get them to her tonight. Thanks, J."

"Anything for a friend."

"If you need something—an art project, a doctor's note, a hall pass . . ."

"I know who to go to, like always. You know what? I can walk myself home from here. Go deliver the paper now. I bet she's grateful for your help, now that she doesn't have to rewrite an essay on two dead dogs."

Case froze. "Aw, man," he said, his face falling. "Is that what *Where the Red Fern Grows* is about?"

I patted his shoulder. "Sorry. We all lose our innocence sooner or later. See you tomorrow."

I left, feeling about as glum as Case did. Why, you ask? After all, didn't I do two successful jobs in one day?

Yes, and they were boring.

When I first started retrieving, I did it to make my mark on Scottsville Middle School. I was tired of people calling me "Rick's little brother" three years after he moved on to high school, so I started taking jobs that used *my* unique skills, talents gained from years of sneaking things (like Halloween candy) from Rick without him finding out, watching movies, and practicing with Case and Hack. I wanted to be remembered as the greatest retrieval specialist Scottsville had ever known. After I left and moved on to high school, maybe even college, kids would still talk about how I'd infiltrated locked rooms as easily as the smell of popcorn. I wouldn't be in anyone's shadow; others would be in mine.

But after the first couple of jobs, I became addicted to the thrill of the chase, loved the fear that I'd get caught. I'd never felt so alert, so awake, so alive, as when I was on a job. I loved the heightened senses that came when I was listening with one ear to a combination lock clicking and with the other for the footsteps of a teacher. I lived for creating a last-minute plan when the teacher decided to eat her lunch in her classroom, blocking my way to her confiscated-technology drawer. I needed it as much as I needed to be known for what I did.

Today's second job—going inside a house, leaving so much to chance—once would have been electrifying. But now it was nothing more than a little fun. The thrill had evaporated when I'd stopped making mistakes that could have gotten me caught, moving from amateur to professional. No more fumbling with my lockpicks, wasting valuable time. No more searching every pocket before finding my client's belongings: I'd learned where papers, wallets, and phones tended to settle. Everything had become a sleepwalk, just going through the practiced motions. As much as I hoped one day I'd get a job that would test my limits and make me feel fear again, I had to admit to myself it probably wouldn't come anytime soon.

I had become too good.

WHEN I GOT HOME, I HOPED
to find an empty couch in front of the TV or maybe
dinner set out on the table since it was almost seven.
Instead I found someone standing outside my door,
checking the time on his cell phone. Back door, that
is. Yeah, sometimes I come in through the back door.
Remember Becca, my nosy neighbor across the street?

My eyes widened in surprise. The guy in front of me
was an eighth grader. "What can I do for you?" I asked.

True, I did the occasional job for the monarchs of the
school, but some of the time they *were* the thieves and con
artists. Most of them were fine, upstanding citizens, but
a few . . . boy, the kind of power that comes with being
the oldest really goes to some people's heads. To have one
show up in my backyard was uncommon. Whatever the
job was, it would be good.

"Are you Jeremy?" the guy asked. He was tall and skinny, with a mouth full of braces. He also had on a short-sleeved shirt that revealed a fading bruise high on his arm. Sports injury, maybe?

"Depends. Why are you here?"

"My name is Mark Chandler," the eighth grader said. "They say you're the best at getting stuff back."

"Who told you that?" It never hurts to be a little cautious in my line of work.

"Lacey Yi. She rides my bus."

I knew Lacey. I'd retrieved some makeup for her. "Okay. What did you lose?"

Mark reached into his back pocket and took out a piece of paper with a rough picture of a key drawn on it. "It's my house key. My mom is out of town, and Dad gave it to me so I could get in while he was at work. I was fiddling with it in math, and Ms. Browning confiscated it."

"Ms. Browning's not usually that hard-nosed. Why didn't she just ask you to put it away?"

Mark shrugged. "She may have done that . . . a few times."

"Say no more. I got it." I studied the picture. The key had teeth on one side and a square top labeled with a black *X*. "The *X*?"

"Um . . . to keep it from being mixed up with our other keys," Mark explained. "My dad's a little scatter-brained, and it's easier for him to label his keys than to try each one. The car key has a red *X*."

"I see. Do you know where the key is now?"

"Yeah. Ms. Browning had trouble opening a drawer and called the janitor. My key was sitting on her desk, and somehow I think my key got mixed up with his. It's in the janitor's closet now."

Easy. No one monitored the janitor's closet, and the door had only one simple lock. But something tugged at me. "Why not talk to the office? If it was that important, they'd understand. Why come to me?"

"I didn't want to risk them calling my dad. It's not the first time I've lost one of his keys."

"Uh-huh." Mark was hiding something. I could tell by the way he met my eyes too easily and by his slightly embarrassed smile. It was practiced, like he wanted me to see him as the victim.

It's not unusual, though. That practiced look appears on about a third of my clients, the ones who are hiring me on behalf of someone else. I bet it wasn't Mark's key; it probably belonged to a girl he was trying to impress. Like Case's job. It would explain why he wouldn't go to the office. Lots of my clients lie to me about how they lost the item, but as long as I could find it where they said, I didn't really care.

"If you lost your key, how did you get back into your house after school today?"

Mark gaped, and I smiled. Hiding something. Definitely for a girl. I decided to help him out. "The back door was open?" I suggested.

He sagged, relieved. "Yeah. I was lucky today, but I'm not sure I will be tomorrow."

"Right. Are you sure it's in the janitor's closet?"

"Pretty sure. Can the great Jeremy Wilderson get my key back?"

I sighed. It would be easy, easier than the job Case gave me. But a guy works what he gets. The more clients, the more my reputation would grow, and the more I could help people. "When do you need it?"

"As soon as possible. My dad won't remember he gave it to me until he needs it, but that could be soon."

I grinned. "Doesn't he have a copy?"

Mark fidgeted. "Yeah, he does . . . but I don't think it's marked. He'll remember."

Retrieving the key would be a sleepwalk. "I can have it for you by tomorrow morning," I said. "Before school."

Mark smiled, revealing blue-banded teeth. "Great! Should I meet you here?"

"No, meet me at the elementary school's playground. It's closer to school."

"Okay. Oh, I almost forgot. What's your price?"

I shook my head. "No price. Just pass my name on to someone else who needs my kind of expertise. But if it would make you feel better, I enjoy chocolate cake."

Before the first bell has rung and the first bus has arrived, when the halls are empty and a retrieval specialist can work without interruption . . . is there any better moment?

Okay, so maybe later in the afternoon—getting up early felt worse than I thought it would. At least there was one perk: Even if there was anyone around to see me, no one would give a student grief for coming to school half an hour *early*, especially if that student arrived with his teacher mother. But the only creature to care about me poking around the janitor's closet was a spider scurrying along the wall.

I had seen the door many times, but the contents of the janitor's closet were an enticing mystery. A mystery guarded by a metal door that would be impossible to break down—but who needed to break down a door when it had one easily pickable lock? After examining the lock for five seconds, I knew for sure. Sleepwalk.

The job wasn't worth my time. I yawned and wished I hadn't gotten up quite so early.

At the moment the janitor worked somewhere else in the building, sweeping floors, scrubbing toilets—whatever janitors usually do before the kids arrive. I had more time than it takes to run a mile on the school track to open this door and find Mark's key. But I didn't need the time it takes to run even one lap. After months of experience, I knew to try the door before using my picks on it. Guess what? It was unlocked. Score one for Wilderson.

I'd like to tell you that I had to defeat a laser grid and pressure switches. I'd like to say I used a grappling hook to beat a hasty retreat once I had the key. But the truth is, most jobs aren't that dramatic. I do have a grappling hook, but the Boy Scout uniform I bought at Goodwill as a disguise gets more wear. For most jobs, I walk in, retrieve the package, and walk out. Grab-and-go.

The key hung on its own ring, separate from the janitor's other keys. I expected that; a lost key would have a ring and maybe a key chain of its own. But the ring with Mark's key dangled from its own hook, which was odd. Why wouldn't the janitor have handed it over to the office once he realized it wasn't his? Maybe he figured it was one of his many, many keys, but didn't believe it enough to thread it back on his key ring. No other explanation made sense, since not even I had known what the inside of the janitor's closet looked like, and I'd been checking on it for months.

Mark was waiting for me at the elementary school playground across the street, leaning against the tiny jungle gym, when I arrived with the key. He straightened up when he saw me.

"Do you have it?"

I looked around first—I have to assume Becca is always watching me—and then pulled the key out of my pocket. "Depends. Is this it?"

Mark's eyes widened. "My key! That's it. That's definitely it." He put out his hand and I dropped the key into it.

"I can't tell you how much this means to me," Mark said. "My dad would have killed me if he found out I'd lost this."

"You be surprised how many of my clients face that kind of problem. But now you have it back. No harm done." I watched his face, trying to figure out what secret he was hiding about the key and hoping it was funny. Sometimes my clients tell me the truth straight-out after the job's done.

Not this time, though. Mark's fingers closed around the key, and he just smiled at me. The smile seemed strange, forced. "You really are the best, aren't you?"

"So they tell me."

"Well, long live the king. What's today, Wednesday? I guess I'll see you in school."

"Maybe," I said, and we returned, satisfied, to Scottsville Middle.

So what if the job has become boring? I made myself think. *So what if everything is just a grab-and-go for people who won't even tell me the whole story?* It felt good to help those needy students that Becca would hang out to dry because they broke a rule or two. It really did. And if I made myself a legend doing it, well, I wasn't complaining.

But if that job had been as simple as I thought it was then, I wouldn't be telling you about it now.

WHEN DONE RIGHT, LUNCH-
time can be better than a class spent watching a movie.
It's free from intense teacher supervision and, since
moving up from elementary school also means graduat-
ing from recess, it's the only time students are allowed
to let loose and have a little fun. This tends to make the
cafeteria pretty loud, but that's good for me: Any eaves-
droppers (read, Becca) would have a hard time hearing
what we talk about at my table. Like how Case's job
worked out.

"After you left, I delivered the essay," Case said as I
spooned peaches into my mouth. He had on a Patriots
jersey.

"What's her name?" Hack said as he sat down next to
me. As usual after a recent grounding, he looked oddly
groomed. His red hair was combed and parted and his

glasses were free of fingerprints. His mom was a sucker for a good show.

"That's what I asked," I said. "He won't tell."

Case rolled his eyes. "It's not your business. Oh, and how did the Bethesda job go, J?"

I shrugged. "Grab-and-go. Dragged Adam's backpack into the bathroom and found the wallet inside. Carrie was waiting in the band room. Your job for me last night was more interesting."

"Sounds like the Yi job."

"Kind of. The Yi job involved a purse, not a backpack, but yeah. Becca stopped me in the hall, by the way."

Hack coughed. "And you're still alive?"

"Of course. He's sitting right here. But that reminds me." Case handed Hack and me matching hall passes signed by Vice Principal Woodrow. "They just changed styles; your old ones are expired now."

"Thanks, man." I looked at the professional-looking pass. "I always need one of these."

"I've got a whole bundle in my locker, for anyone who needs them."

"I may send some clients your way. I know Cricket has gotten a lot of use out of his old pass."

"I hope you understand how difficult it was this time," Case said, cutting his pizza with a fork and knife. "Woodrow must have bought new pens; the black ink on the original split into a different array of colors than it used to when I dipped a sample in water. I spent hours trying every black pen in my dad's desk until I got one that matched."

"Oh, come on, Case," Hack said. "Why couldn't you use just any black pen? No one cares if you match the ink exactly as long as you get the handwriting right."

"I don't know," I said. "I saw the peer mediators spritzing hall passes with the water fountain this morning, checking for fakes."

"Ha-ha, J." Case stashed his fork over his ear.

I pointed. "Not a pencil, man."

"What?" Case asked as Hack took the fork and waved it. "Oh. Anyway, is it so bad if I take pride in my work?"

"And we don't?" Hack and I chorused.

"Hack, if you took any pride in your work, you wouldn't leap right into firewalls without planning out what you'll do if they spit you right out." Case stabbed a bite of pizza with his fork. "You know you wouldn't be grounded so often if you thought things through."

Hack grinned and pushed his glasses up his nose. "Maybe I should take your lead and obsess over inks."

"Be careful," I warned. "You may have doomed us to a lecture on how you can tell the quality of a black ink by the cyan-to-red ratio."

Case glared at us. "Magenta. Not red."

Hack widened his eyes in horror. "Oh no. I beg you, have mercy."

"Better settle down for a nap now," I said. "It'll get harder once he starts the passionate speech on gradations."

Case groaned and took a sip of milk. "And, J, here's *your* problem. You don't take anything seriously. And you're out of your mind."

I tilted my head. "Can't argue with you there, but which of my many insanities are you referring to? Oh, thank you," I said as loaded-wallet Carrie dropped a plastic-wrapped slice of chocolate cake in front of me. She smiled as she walked away, and I waved. "Pleasure doing business with you."

"Great," Hack said, pulling the cake his way. "Payday."

"Hang on. Let me unwrap it first." I grabbed the cake and started unraveling the sticky plastic wrap. "I can't be that insane if I keep getting paid."

"Oh yeah?" Hack said, picking up his fork. "What makes you insane is that you work at *this* school."

I balled up the plastic wrap. "So? You guys work at Burdick and the elementary and high schools. And I know Case takes jobs at Da Vinci Academy."

Case snorted. "Those schools don't have any of our parents teaching there. Or a shot-putter detective named

Becca who has a personal vendetta against one Jeremy Wilderson. Hey, Hack. Pass that here."

"'Vendetta,' huh?" I said as Hack slid my cake to Case. "I guess someone's having a vocab test today."

"Seriously, J. Keep this up, sooner or later you'll leave evidence. And then she'll catch you." Case took a bite of the cake. "Wow. I think this icing has raspberry jam mixed in."

"Let me try." Hack scooped up a fourth of the slice and shoved it in his mouth. "Oh man. So much better than the cream-filled snack cakes you usually get."

"Yeah, Carrie has good taste. I wonder if she made this herself." I pulled the cake closer and took a bite before my friends could finish it off for me. It was one of the better payments I'd received for a job.

Hack glanced across the lunchroom at Becca. "There she goes. Taking more pictures for her files on all of us."

We all looked. Becca lowered her camera and glared at me.

"We've been over this. She doesn't keep files on us," Case argued.

"Then how come she knew I was the one who rick-rolled the school during morning announcements the day before spring break?"

"Because everyone knows that," I said.

"She follows us everywhere," Hack said. "Taking pictures. I caught her watching me in the computer lab. The snitch was just peering in through the window. When I looked at her, she smiled and took a picture. For the file. Next thing I know, I get moved to a computer with a screen that faces the teacher."

"That's nothing," Case said. "Ms. Grant talked to me in December about missing paints. The snitch was investigating and told her that I had been taking the paints home with me. Stealing them. Why would I want paints that people dip dirty brushes in when I have my own at home?"

"How come you never told me about that?" I asked.

"Nonissue. The paints turned up the next day. Someone had stored them in the wrong cupboard."

"But why would she suspect you?"

Hack rocked in his chair. "Because we're your friends, and she hates you. We've seen how she jumps you in the hallway. Imagine how much she'd squeeze us if we didn't only take jobs at other schools."

Case laughed. "*Squeeze* us? Dude, what does that even *mean*?"

Don't be fooled by Case and Hack's constant bickering; they would do anything for each other. Once, when Hack got called down to the office for breaking into the school's website, Case forged a parent's note and got him out. Just thinking about it makes my throat feel like Becca has it in a choke hold. In a good way.

But at least Case and Hack's going at each other got them both off my back. Who cares where I work? The kids here need my services just as much as at the charter school and the elementary and high schools. I'm not going to let some tiny girl scare me away, no matter how good her arm is.

"Dude," Hack said, pointing at Case's jersey. "Pick a team. Doesn't matter which one. Just pick one."

Case held up his gloves. "I may admire a lot of teams, but you know it's the Eagles. Now and forever."

"Really? Them? They never win!"

"They would if we ever finished a game of Madden. Don't you think it's time you stop hacking your mom's e-mail? You just keep getting grounded!"

"Yeah," I cut in, glad the conversation's focus had fallen away from me. "Besides, didn't we promise to use our skills to help people?"

"It was just a little practice," Hack said. "Mom got a new security system. What, was I not supposed to try to break through it? But yeah, I need to lie low. Mom said she'll send me to live with Dad if I try it again. She says that will straighten me out."

Hack's dad tests the security systems of big companies by pretending to be a hacker. He tries to break in, and if he can do it, the company needs to fix their firewalls. Oh yeah, living with his dad will totally straighten Hack out.

I've only seen Paul Heigel Sr. once, at one of Hack's birthday parties before his parents split. He looked like an older version of Hack, as if the body came package deal with the name. Red hair, glasses, muscular build. If I gambled, I'd bet good money that Hack will wind up in the same job, testing electronic security. That, or in prison.

I was about to make some comment about Hack, Case, and me being the school's Future Jailbirds of America club when something caught my eye. Call it chance, call it destiny, or call it my fine-tuned senses, but I noticed the exact moment when Becca left her usual perch—where she had glared at me all through lunch— and left the cafeteria. Ignoring the teacher with the sign-out sheet as she went.

Interesting, very interesting. Becca was a stickler for rules; what was so important that she didn't want anyone asking questions? Whatever it was, I had to see for myself.

"Excuse me, but duty calls," I said, standing up and tilting my head at the hall.

"Have fun on the toilet!" Hack called.

Case dropped his head into his hands and groaned. "You'd make a Neanderthal look refined."

Sheesh. Just because someone's working on a fake Picasso in his room doesn't make him the authority on culture.

Dodging the teacher on sign-out-sheet duty was easy—his head dipped with exhaustion, and Hack chose that moment to toss my lunch tray to the floor. A useful distraction, if my least favorite of their repertoire. At least I'd finished the cake before beginning this chase.

Following Becca was harder. Whenever I stepped too loud, she stopped and looked behind her, forcing me to hide behind lockers, doors, anything. But, step by nerve-racking step, I got through it and ended up outside the teachers' lounge.

Most kids think the teachers' lounge is some kind of theme park that kids aren't allowed to know about. That's not true. It has a TV, a refrigerator, a well-used coffee machine, and some couches. Draped, of course, with dead-exhausted teachers and staff. Now, how I first got inside, *that* is a good story. It involves a ferret.

But that's for another time. This particular afternoon, a couple of the normally dead-exhausted teachers stood outside the open door, talking in hushed tones.

Becca was crouched down the hall from them,

hidden behind a row of lockers. I lurked around the corner; if I craned my head around, I could see her and the teachers. If I didn't, I stayed perfectly hidden and could hear just fine.

"Are you going to tell them?" one teacher asked. A woman, but she taught eighth grade so I didn't know her name.

"No! If the kids knew the key was out there, free for the taking, we'd have a real crisis on our hands." Her companion was Coach Cread, the gym teacher. A decent human being most of the time, but hard on us poor, innocent kickballs. I mean children.

"You shouldn't be so quick to judge. I'm just saying, there are hundreds of them. One of them might find the key before the end of school tomorrow, and then the janitor would have it back. No harm done."

"The final word is no. That comes from Jacob himself. None of the kids are to know the master key is missing. At least for a few days while we search."

Jacob. That would be Principal McDuff. Wait, did he say master key? Not *the* master key! I must have heard wrong. I twisted my neck so my ear stuck out around the corner.

"I won't argue with Jacob," the female teacher said. "Not over this. But I think we should still tell them."

"How about this? We tell Becca, get her working on it for now."

What did I say? Teachers' darling.

"Already have. She'll give it to Jacob if she finds it. What are we going to do in the meantime until the key is found? What if a student forgets his combination?"

Coach Cread probably had some kind of response for her, but I didn't hear it. So it *was* the master key that was lost, the key that would open any locker door in the school. I was torn between hoping the teachers found it before the day ended and wishing I would find it before they did. It was, after all, the Holy Grail of retrieving.

I wanted to ditch the rest of lunch, go to the janitor's closet, and scan the floor for the key, but a little dark-haired fiend ended that dream. Before I could think, Becca's hands were clutching my shirt as she rammed my head into the wall.

"Owww . . . ," I moaned, but Becca isn't known for her sympathy.

"Look what I found," she said, smirking. "Taking pride in your work?"

"According to some, pride in one's work isn't the luxury of the insane." I rubbed my head. "Can I help you with something, or can I go to the nurse now?"

"You should be in the cafeteria."

"So should you."

"Some things are more important than lunch," she said. "But let's not waste time, Wilderson. Where's the key?"

"Lost, or so I hear," I said. "The teachers are worried. Too bad this school doesn't have a detective who can go out and find it for us—hey, wait a second," I said. "I have a great idea. Why don't you get your hands off me and go take this case?"

"I already have," Becca said, and her grip on my collar tightened. I didn't think hands could close that tightly. My throat felt like it does when I think about Case bailing out Hack.

"And," she continued, "I know who the culprit is. You're pretty proud of yourself, aren't you? From now on you won't have to worry about leaving evidence."

"Please. I only leave evidence if I want to."

"Whatever." Becca let go, and I doubled over, acting as if I were gasping for air. "It's not your fault, Wilderson."

"It's not?"

"I can imagine how tempting the master key would be for you. The key that opens any student's locker—it would make your thieving so much easier."

"How many times do we need to go over this? I'm not a thief."

Becca didn't seem to hear me. "Your mom's a teacher here and you come in early all the time. You know when the janitor's not near his closet. It would be so easy for you to walk in, find the key marked with an *X*, and leave. No one the wiser. Well, except for me." She smiled.

"Good luck with that theory, considering I'm not a thie—wait, did you say it was marked with an *X*?"

Becca smiled like she was laying a trap. "Black *X*. Square top. Seen anything like that lately?"

She knew. I knew she knew. But she had no photos, no evidence except my confession, and I'd rather lick the school-bus floor than give her that. I had to stay free to make Mark pay for what he'd done.

I *knew* he'd been hiding something! I shouldn't have assumed it was something innocent just because the job was easy.

"I'm confused," I said. "Why mark the key with an *X*? Isn't it kind of like writing 'Steal me' on the master key?"

Becca lowered her eyes. "The janitor marked it because he has to pull it out of the key ring so many times. It's faster when he doesn't have to scrutinize every single one."

"'Scrutinize.' Good vocab word. Are you, by any chance, in Casey Kingston's language arts class?"

"Do I look like I associate with your crooked friends?"

I looked her over. "No."

"Lunch is almost over. Where's the key?"

"I don't have it," I replied, the picture of honesty.

Becca stepped back, staring at me. "Whatever. I can't hold you here, but remember this: Now you've gone too far. I'll find the key, and I'll prove you took it. And when I do, you'll finally know what in-school suspension looks like."

"I've peeked through the window. It didn't look that bad."

"*Yours* will be bad," she assured me. "I'll make sure of it." And with that she walked away.

And Case thinks I'm *nuts,* I thought. At least I don't go around threatening people in the hallway.

But when I thought about Mark and how he'd used me to steal the master key, I decided it might be time to give it a try.

I FOUND MARK IN THE EIGHTH-

grade hallway after the last bell rang. He was leaning against his locker, chatting with friends, all innocence. He laughed, flashing braces, and held his head with a jauntiness that made my blood boil.

"Excuse me," I said, pushing through a crowd of guys twice as tall as me and double my weight. "Coming through. Need to see a man about a job."

This particular crowd of eighth-grade guys looked like they wanted to lodge me under a desk like chewed gum. For a moment I felt as though I'd jumped into shark-infested water wearing swim trunks made of raw tuna. All these big guys . . . and I knew nothing about Mark. Could he be some kind of kingpin with an army of goons behind him? If so, how did I not know about him? Was he the kind of bad guy who hung back and ran his empire by manipulating others into doing his dirty work?

But then a couple of the guys walked past Mark and his friends, and one of them shot a hand out and into Mark, slamming him into the lockers. The guys didn't apologize, not that I expected them to, but they didn't laugh, either.

Cheap fun. That's what Mark was to them. Now I understood the bruise I'd seen on Mark's arm.

I cleared my throat and waved. Mark looked up and grinned. "Hey, Jeremy! Good to see you so soon. Come on over here."

"You hang with a tough crowd," I said as I walked through the pack of big, smelly dudes to where Mark stood.

He smiled and nodded, missing my sarcasm. "That's right." He raised a hand for a high five that went ignored by the other eighth graders until one of his friends tapped it. Even so, the delusional jerk looked as pleased as if a high school quarterback had begged to be his best friend. Let me tell you, Rick has enough friends without having to beg for manipulative eighth-grade lowlifes.

How on *earth* did I not see this lunatic coming?

"I don't mean to be a pain, but can you and I have a little privacy to talk?" I tilted my head at Mark's buddies, who were still milling around.

Mark nodded and laid the sweet charm on his associates: *Hey, I'll see you later, got to finish up some business, you know how sixth graders can be,* all the usual lines. He still had that glow around him, that arrogance of someone who's gotten away with a crime. I knew it well; all the people who ripped off my clients had the same glow. I guess Mark hadn't looked into my eyes yet and seen that the game was up.

"So," Mark said, putting a hand on my shoulder, "what can I do for you? Oh, wait. I remember. You want payment." He dug into his jeans and pulled out a crumpled green bill. Stretching it to full length in front of my face, he added, "No chocolate cake for you, my friend. You're worth a little more than that."

I froze, mesmerized by Andrew Jackson. Most clients paid me for my services—it made them feel honest—but payment usually came in the form of chocolate cake or IOUs for future favors. An actual greenback, and twenty dollars at that, shone just like the clip-on waterproof flashlight it would buy.

I closed my eyes and shook off the spell. "I'm sorry," I said, looking up past the money to Mark's face, "but I can't accept that."

"Not enough?"

"No, it's plenty." Oh, so much money. I could put it

toward a real set of night-vision goggles. "It's just that the job isn't finished."

Threatening an eighth grader isn't something one does lightly, and I would be lying if I said I didn't take comfort in the fact that he was a nobody to his classmates. "You hired me to retrieve a stolen key, and that's what I'm going to do."

Mark chuckled and folded his arms. He stared at me, releasing short bursts of laughter as if that would make everything I said a joke. After a minute his grin faded. "You're not serious."

"I seriously am."

"Look. You did good, kid. Take the money and revel in a job well done. The master key. Kids will be talking about that for weeks. Well, maybe days. At least until they have something better to talk about." He laughed again.

I bristled at him calling me "kid" but moved past it. "No one knows about the master key, so I doubt they'll talk about it. But that's good news. It's not too late; give me back the key and I'll return it, no one the wiser." I didn't actually think he'd accept my offer, but it was worth a shot. For good measure I played the guilt card. "Stealing is wrong."

Mark rolled up the twenty and shoved it back in his

pocket. "Like I believe you mean that. You're the school's biggest thief . . . or you *were*."

I wanted to argue that retrieving wasn't stealing, but you can't argue with crazy. "What are your plans for the key?"

"What does that matter to you?"

"It always matters to me when a new . . . thief . . . encroaches on my territory."

Thief. The word felt dirty in my mouth. But Mark, through his trickery, had turned me into what I had fought against since starting at Scottsville Middle. Like it or not, until the key was returned, I was a thief.

As I spoke, I watched Mark's face. Dealing with Becca had taught me that even the barest twitch of the eyebrows could speak volumes. And believe me, she caught every unspoken word. Mark never betrayed shame or guilt, but his eyes widened, just a twitch, during my last sentence.

"You're thinking of making a name for yourself as Scottsville's new thief," I said, trying to channel Becca's annoying smugness.

Mark smiled. "Why not? If you can do it, how hard can it be?"

"I'll tell you, it's pretty easy when you have a *master key* doing all the work for you." I shook my head. "Taking the easy way out like that? You disgust me. Have you no professional pride?"

"Maybe not," Mark said. "But pride is worth nothing. We know that. We know what *really* matters."

"And what is that?" I was so sick of this kid.

"Being untouchable." Mark's smile had slipped away. He folded an arm across his chest, resting his hand on the bruise on his arm. "With all the powerful people you've stolen from in the last year, someone should have dropped you facedown in the Dumpster behind the gym, or at least complained to a teacher. But that hasn't happened. No one touches you, Jeremy. They all know that if they mess with you, you can take everything they own and reveal secrets they might not even know they had. The power you have makes them afraid of you. Your name, your reputation, is your shield."

Mark was right: I hadn't been picked on or sent to the principal or anything you might expect after retrieving from so many scary people. I'd been so focused on doing my work and avoiding Becca that I hadn't even noticed. Was he also right that it was because I, with my reputation preceding me, was scarier than the biggest, meanest bully in the lunchroom? That thought made my stomach clench.

"Let me guess," I said. "You think using the key to

rob everyone will give you a big, scary reputation and no one will ever bother you again."

Mark narrowed his eyes. "I *know* it will. Fear is the best protection a guy can have, and once treasures start vanishing from people's lockers without any evidence of a break-in, I'll inspire that fear."

"Hard to do that when no one knows you're the one stealing from them."

"Oh, they'll know. It's all about timing. I'll let them stew in their fear for a little while, and then I'll start a rumor and everyone will know enough to call me a thief. They'll call me a *master* thief. No one will touch me. But you, little Jeremy Wilderson, will fade into obscurity. The king is dead; long live the—"

"Shut up." I worked to keep my teeth from grinding. "Obscurity? I'm going to be here for two more years. You don't even have two weeks."

Mark grinned. "Nothing like going out with a bang. A bang, by the way, that will echo through high school. People think that middle school is the end of it. They're wrong. It's only the beginning. What I start here will build in high school until everyone knows who I am."

This guy was a moron. "You can't start anything when you can't even use the key. It will be months before the heat dies down enough that no one connects the key with the thefts."

An evil glint lit Mark's eye. "Good thing I didn't steal the key."

That stopped me cold. Clever guy, using me to steal the master key. He could go ahead with his plans because every scrap of evidence left at the scene—if I left any—would lead back to me. I didn't leave evidence; I don't unless I want to. But I also had a reputation as sticky-fingered. If the other students lost precious objects, they'd blame me first.

"Why do you think I'm waiting to reveal myself? First you'll have to get caught," Mark said. "The big, scary thief will have fallen, and no one will fear you anymore. But then I'll rise, using the key to steal on a level you never had the courage to try, and they'll transfer that fear to me, the new thief in town."

Never had the courage? Was that what he thought was holding me back from being the criminal he clearly wanted to be?

I'd lost my patience with this idiot. "And let me guess: When you release these rumors and tell everyone that you're the thief, you're not going to mention using the master key, are you? No, that will be your secret." I shook my head. "Come on. You're no thief. You hired me to get that key to frame me, sure, but you couldn't do it yourself. You don't have a thief's brain, and you certainly don't have the mojo to pull off a heist of any size, let alone the big score you're dreaming of, without cheating. But I do. Everyone says I'm the best at what I do, and they're right. You should be scared of me, because there is nowhere you can hide that key that I can't find it."

A slight flicker of fear tripped over Mark's face, and I knew I had him. Then he smiled and said, "Good luck with that. As people start losing stuff, I wonder how long you'll have to track down one tiny key before they haul you in." He turned and left.

I was really getting sick of people ending conversations with me by walking away, but I wasn't stupid enough to follow him. I bit my lip in frustration and walked to the seventh-grade hall to wait for Mom.

I KNOW I SAID THAT I WANTED

an exciting job, but this was becoming *too* exciting. Mark had the key and was not afraid to use it. The next day I'd be busy with kids looking to hire me to retrieve the stuff they lost, and on top of that I'd have to work on a plan to outwit Mark.

I meant what I said to Mark: The job wasn't done yet. This whole mess was my fault because I'd stolen the master key, so it was my responsibility to take it back. It's just what I do: retrieve stolen property and return it to its rightful owner. Mom would be so proud of me if she knew about my work.

But I wasn't blind to the challenges.

I would have to find the key, a three-inch-long piece of metal that Mark could have duct-taped into his armpit for all I knew (and I wouldn't put it past him). Then

I would have to return everything he took without getting caught by him or any of the teachers, who wouldn't understand if stolen goods turned up in my backpack. And the clock was ticking. The job was a lot to handle. Too much for one guy.

Ask Case and Hack? No. Definitely not. They would help me, but as long as the key was missing, my back had a target painted on it. If Case and Hack got involved and helped me poke around, they'd get that same target on theirs. Mark could easily point the finger at me. It would only take a few more words to implicate my friends. This wasn't dealing with a few dollars of lunch money; this job had high stakes.

Also, if Mark's plan worked and he started to accumulate street cred as he committed his crime spree, he could get a few more friends. Big friends. Nasty friends. Friends who liked to hurt people. I was certain that Mark would send those friends after me, and anyone who helped me, if I tried to get the key back. Giving up the master key to Mark was not an option. I could put myself in harm's way over a mistake I made, but I wouldn't ever put Case and Hack in that position. No, Case and Hack had to stay in the dark on this one.

I wouldn't need a forger or a hacker for this job. Hack could keep working on getting himself ungrounded, and

Case could stay busy being art class's golden boy and working on his submission to the county's summer art competition. (Remember the Picasso I mentioned? That's not it.)

But I needed help. Someone athletic enough to handle goons, but smart enough to play whatever con was needed. I had some contacts in the underground who might help—kids who tended to know where stolen stuff ended up—but they were thieves, and the master key was too tempting a prize. I had to find someone honest, someone the teachers would trust over Mark if he tried to implicate them in the theft, and someone who wouldn't take the package and run once the job was over. Someone who might put rules above everything, but cares about student welfare above her own personal gain.

I only knew one person who fit the description. And after Mom drove me home, I walked across the street to talk to her.

"Hey, Becca," I said when she opened her door. "Got a moment?"

"If you're here to confess, I've got all the time in the world."

I peered into her house. "Are you home alone?"

"Dad's working on his closing remarks and Mom's following a lead on a breaking-and-entering case. Why?"

I took the liberty of walking into her front hall.

"Because I don't want to be overheard by the lawyer and the cop."

Yep. Lawyer and cop. And Becca's their unholy offspring.

She glared at me. "Rude, much?"

"Can you close the door?"

Becca did as I asked, but her face expressed how much she would have loved an excuse to throw me out the window just like Miss Trunchbull from *Matilda*. After she shut the door, she turned to me with folded arms. "Well?"

I took a deep breath and exhaled slowly. "All right, it was me. I stole the master key. I'm your thief."

Becca beamed like Christmas had come early and Santa had given her the stun gun she wanted. "I never thought you'd actually give yourself up," she said, and laughed. "Hold on. Let me get my camera so I can capture this moment and keep it forever."

I grabbed her arm as she spun to go upstairs. "I'm not done yet," I said. "There's a lot more to this. We might want to sit down."

She led me to the kitchen table, where we sat and I told her about Mark and how he used me to get the key. Becca didn't look sympathetic; her eyes and the tilt of her mouth screamed that I'd had it coming. When I explained Mark's plan to steal from the lockers, her composure cracked. But when I presented my proposal, it shattered completely.

"No way am I helping you with any thief work!"

"Hear me out, Becca." Neither of us was sitting anymore. She paced the hardwood floor, circling the table, and I followed, trying to make her see the sense of joining forces.

"Not going to happen, Wilderson. I've got what I want. You said you stole the key. You're going to do time in detention, and I'll be there to see it. Maybe even try to get everything you've done on your permanent record. Problem solved."

"Not quite."

She stopped pacing and looked at me. I grinned. "You don't have me."

"You confessed."

"Maybe. But if I did, it was off the record. I didn't say anything in front of an authority figure, I didn't write it down, and I didn't do anything stupid like, say, let myself get captured saying it. And proof is everything, isn't it, in your business?"

Becca's mouth opened, and she swelled like she was going to yell at me, but nothing came out. She knew I was right. She had nothing but what I was willing to give her.

"And suppose you did get me on record," I added.

"Best-case scenario: You'll have me, but Mark will have the key. And Scottsville will be trapped in a massive crime spree. You'll have solved nothing."

For a moment Becca looked unsure, but before long the old hard-boiled façade returned. She leaned against the table, facing me. "I know Mark has the key. All I have to do is turn him in to the principal."

I sat down and leaned back in the kitchen chair, two legs tipped off the floor, and looked up at her. "It will be Mark's word against yours. And if he doesn't have the key on his person, you'll have no proof."

Becca pushed back on my chair, sending me crashing to the floor with a thud. "I should drag you into school and force you to confess in front of the principal. Then they'd know you stole the key and that Mark has it now."

Flat on my back, I waited until the pain subsided before giving her my best innocent expression. "Imagine how silly you would look when I said I had no idea what you were talking about."

Silence. Becca walked around the table as I stood up and returned the chair to its place. She sat down across from me with the sun streaming through the window behind her.

"This," she said. "This is why I hate you. You think

you can get away with anything. And what's worse? You. Always. *Can.*" She slammed her fists down on the table.

"Yeah, Mark said something like that. He wants people to fear him like they fear me."

Becca leaned back. Her face was shadowed, but I saw her smiling. "Oh, *that's* what you think it is."

"That's what Mark thinks." Personally, I'd rather not be feared. I hated the thought that Mark was right and the only reason I was good at stopping bad guys was because I was the nastiest monster out there. That's not who I wanted to be.

"Let me tell you something, Wilderson," Becca said in a mild tone that made me think this was a bed-time story I'd prefer not to hear. "Remember the Rance McLeod job?"

I thought back. "Stolen skateboard?"

Becca nodded. "That's the one."

Rance McLeod, seventh grader, stole a skateboard from sixth grader Jake Piedmont. It was a simple job, one of my first, back in October.

"I'd been noticing some strange things going on since school started," Becca said. "People losing things and then getting them back. Doors unlocked when they should have been locked. I saw Jake without the skateboard in the morning, and then I saw him leaving school with it."

"What can I say? I work fast."

"I talked to Jake, and he gave me your name," Becca said. "I investigated, but I found no evidence of theft. So I took Rance's statement. He told me he knew you retrieved the skateboard from his locker, and that you were behind a number of similar cases. But do you know what?"

"What?" The word was a trap; I shouldn't have said it.

"When I asked Rance to come with me and tell Principal McDuff what you did, testify against your vicious rule-breaking, he refused. Why? Because he said you'd once retrieved a retainer for him, and he might need you to do it again one day." Becca bared her teeth and leaned over the table. "People aren't scared of *you*, Wilderson; they're scared that one day you won't be there to help them when they need you."

"Oh." I leaned, one-handed, on the table and thought, *Now, that's better than being feared.* "That's good."

"No, it's disgusting!" Becca stood up and jabbed a finger at me. "Why should *you* get away with crime when no one else can? Why are *you* above the rules? Who made *you* so special? And then, after I talked to Rance, you had the *gall* to rub your illegal security in my face by asking me to join you! Someone needs to make you pay, just like everyone pays, and if no one else will put together a case against you, then I guess I'll do it!"

Becca was shaking. Her pointed finger hung in the air, a physical accusation. For a moment, neither of us spoke.

"Go ahead," I said. "Put together that case against me. But not right now. Mark is a bigger threat to the school than I am, and even though you hate me, I think you know that."

Becca sank back into her chair, folded her arms, and nodded once.

I nodded back. "I might have a plan to get the key back, and it won't work without you. Together we can return the key to the school, pin Mark with the crime, and go off to summer vacation with not a care in the world."

"But to do that, we'd have to break the rules."

"A few, maybe."

"Lie. Act dishonestly."

"Definitely."

She shook her head. "Nope. Mom says the law's the law for a reason. People who break it only hurt other people and themselves. I agree." She glared at me. "That's why no one should be above the law."

"Oh, *now* you're Little Miss Straight Arrow. Where was that moral compass when you snuck out of the cafeteria to spy on the teachers?"

She turned red. "The teachers gave me the case."

"So you were spying on them? Afraid they didn't give you all the details?"

Becca slammed her fist on the table. Just one fist this time. "That was for the greater good. Not that you'd care about that."

"So you're above the law when it suits your needs, but when I bend a few rules to help someone, I'm Scottsville's Most Wanted?"

Becca glowered, but I continued before she could argue. "This *is* for the greater good. You know we can't let Mark keep that key. I'm not going to ask you to pick locks or climb through windows."

"What are you going to ask me to do?"

"Pardon?"

Now Becca leaned forward, hands clasped. Bet she saw that on some cop show. "I don't think you came to me just for help with a job. What's in this for you?"

I waited for her to answer her own question. When she didn't, I exploded. "Immunity, okay? I don't want you to turn me in. You know that's what I want."

"Yeah, but I wanted to hear you say it." Becca shook her head. "Untouchable Wilderson. Nothing ever sticks to him."

"If it helps, consider this community service."

Becca nodded. I could see the wheels turning in

her head. "Okay, Wilderson. It's a deal. If we get the key back, you walk on this one. Just this one, and *if* we get the key back. If not, I'm bringing you in. And don't expect a pass for any other jobs you take on after this."

"Deal."

"I also have a couple of conditions."

I sighed. Of course she did. "What?"

"First, no stealing. None. Not while we work . . . together." She looked like she was going to throw up. "I'm not getting tangled up in one of your dirty schemes."

"I don't steal. I retrieve."

"None of that either, then. Just the key. You have my permission to grab that as long as you hand it over to me."

I shook my head. "Just the key? Are you crazy? Mark's out there with a key that opens any locker in the school. He's not going to wait around to use it. I'm going to get flooded with clients the minute I set foot in school, and you're telling me that I can't help them while we do this?"

Becca folded her arms. "No deal, no help."

I simmered. I needed her help. "Fine. Deal. What else?"

"You run everything you plan to do past me. You don't pick up a penny in the cafeteria before I hear about it."

She had me, and she knew it. "You're annoying, you know that?"

Becca glared at me. I stuck out my wrist. "Want me to wear a tracking bracelet too?"

"Thought about it. They're too expensive." Becca smirked. "I'm excited now. I get to see the great Jeremy Wilderson in action and learn all his tricks. I'll know what evidence to look for next time I investigate one of your heists."

I revived the wide-eyed look of innocence. "How do you know I haven't seen the light and mended my wicked ways?"

"You can put away the sappy face. I know you too well."

"Ooh, really?" I leaned forward.

"Well enough to know that believing you'll stop stealing is like believing a fox will stop raiding chicken coops."

"You think I'm a fox? I've gotta say, I'm flattered. Was that you checking me out at our last track meet?"

Becca rolled her eyes. "Just lay out this plan you've cooked up."

So I did.

I CAME HOME THAT NIGHT

exhausted. I'd thought my plan was brilliant, but Becca had found the need to criticize every tiny part of it, peppering the whole conversation with name-calling. "Petty thief." "Burglar." "Criminal mastermind." Actually, I kind of liked that last one.

"It involves a lot of sneaking around," Becca said once I'd finished.

"But no stealing. It's not like you're above a little harmless rule-bending."

"This is some Olympic gymnast–caliber bending."

I slammed my hands down on the table, imitating Becca. "I spent the whole ride home coming up with this plan. I think it will work. But please, feel free to speak up if you think you can do better."

"Oh no. I think your plan will work," Becca said.

"Really?"

"Yeah. It's simple. Elegant. Not so many moving parts that it gets complicated, but just enough to keep Mark guessing."

I scrutinized (vocab word) her. She looked serious. "Then why have you been picking apart my ideas?"

"It's fun."

While I contemplated whether turning myself in to Principal McDuff would be less painful than working with Becca, she continued. "Are you sure there's no honest way for me to get the key back?"

"And put me in detention for the rest of my middle school career?" I added, and she smiled and nodded. "In that case," I said, "no. We don't have the time. Besides, what do you care? You're not going to do anything unsavory."

"Being affiliated with you is unsavory. In more ways than one." She fanned the air.

"Really? A body-odor crack? You're better than that, Becca."

It was amid the volley of insults that I took my leave. Going home wasn't much of an improvement: Before I could make it to my room, my center of gravity flip-flopped and I found myself upside down, fingertips brushing the carpet.

"Where have you been, Dr. Evil?" Rick swung me like a pendulum.

"With a friend. Can you put me down now?"

Rick shook me harder, forcing the blood to my face. "Answer honestly, my little criminal friend. Ve have vays of making you talk, and I can do this all day."

I pulled a chunk of lint from the carpet and stuck it to Rick's shorts. "Where's Mom?"

"Picking up Dad. Had enough yet?"

"I see spots."

He laughed. "Just tell me the truth, and you can get back to your death rays."

I closed my eyes and let my body go limp. While Rick's torture was uncomfortable, I could have held out for longer. It's not like I'd never been upside down before; working with grappling hooks and ropes tends to put you in some very unusual positions. But he didn't know that.

"Jeremy. Stop it, Jeremy. Jeremy?"

I didn't respond, and before long Rick gently laid me out on the floor. "Oh my gosh. Breathe." His hands brushed my face.

I grabbed one and bent it back. "You're such a butt-head, Rick."

For a second I thought he was going to kill me, his face got so red. But after he pulled his hand free, he burst out laughing. "Okay, that was a good one. You really had me there. But you have made me look silly and must pay. Rest easy for now, but I promise retaliation will be swift and deadly."

I laughed. Rick was a jerk, but at least he wasn't a boring jerk. "I really was at a friend's."

"No, you were at the Mills's. And that girl is not your friend."

"Like you pay attention to my friends."

"Just watch your back, Dr. Evil, or you might find something stuck in it." Rick flicked the lint from his shorts onto my head and retreated to the kitchen.

I got up and went to my room to begin fine-tuning my plans. Becca and I had talked big picture and arranged her part in getting the master key back from Mark, but I still needed to tighten up some of the nuts and bolts of my part of the job. Like what places I needed to case and when would be the best time to do it.

In a perfect world I could watch Mark and learn what his favorite hiding places were, but I didn't have the time. It was a good thing that Mark was a middle school student and only had a few secure locations anyone would know about. His locker. His backpack. His room at home. I could begin there.

A smart guy like Mark would want to keep the master

key super safe. In those three places the key would be close enough for him to reach it when he wanted, and parents and teachers wouldn't snoop. If I were the thief, my last choice for a hiding place would be my locker. So that would be where I looked first.

Why, you ask? How does that make sense? Hang on, listen a while, and you'll get a feel for my method. If I have to explain everything to you, the story gets boring, and by this point you should know how I feel about boring. So for now all I'll say is that I planned to outwit Mark and search the last place I'd expect the key to be.

See, you're catching on. I'll make a retrieval specialist out of you yet.

Phase one of my three-phase plan was scheduled to begin the very next day. I knew Mark wouldn't waste a single day of his last couple of weeks in middle school, so Becca and I couldn't sit around twiddling our thumbs. What is twiddling, by the way? No one's ever explained that to me.

The next day dawned, a beautiful Thursday morning. A jolt of adrenaline woke me five minutes before my alarm went off. This was it: the job I'd been waiting to do, the one that made me feel alive again. But to do it, I had to trust a straightlaced PI to do her half of the work just right when she wanted nothing more than to cheerfully toss me into eternal detention.

Not a pleasant arrangement.

Mom didn't have to be at school early, so she gave me and Case a ride. During the ride Case, in a 49ers jersey, made veiled comments about how his fake Picasso was coming along; he made it sound like he was doing a project on Picasso's painting style. I could feel my mom's approval hanging in the air like perfumed mist.

At school Case and I met up with Hack just inside the halls. "Hey, anything new?" he asked. "Mom's banned me from the Internet until further notice."

"Yeah, about that." I pulled three comic books out of my backpack. "Sustenance."

"Thanks!" Hack tucked the books into his backpack. "I don't know how much longer I can go before I start annoying Mom just for something to do. What about you, Case?"

"Well, the Picasso's going well," Case said. "I was just telling J about it."

"I meant do you have any comics for me, but your Picasso's good too." Hack adjusted his backpack.

"Why are you doing it, anyway?" I asked. "It sounds like a lot of work, and you have to keep it hidden from your parents and your sisters."

"Yeah," Hack said. "The only people who can ever see it are J and me."

Case shrugged. "I just want to see if I can do it."

More on the Picasso. The original painting is a lesser-known piece that was donated to the local art museum by some tycoon with money coming out of his Ferrari's tailpipe. Case goes there weekly, studying brushstrokes and paint thickness. Granted, he's not going to try to sell his copy as the real deal—he'll be the first to admit that the paint and canvas aren't accurate to Picasso's time, and he's not going to age it—but he's working hard to make it look real. Case won't let anyone see his work, any work, before it's done, so I can't tell you if he's succeeding in this forgery.

"Whatever," Hack said. "Just don't bring it to school. The snitch might bring you down."

Case shivered. "I don't think she'd recognize the piece, but I don't want to find out what she'd do if she suspected forgery. Accusing me of stealing paints was bad enough."

"Is it really a forgery if you aren't trying to pass it off as the real thing?" I asked.

"Becca Mills will say it is." Case shuddered. "And she could make my life miserable for a long time. That girl has an unnatural knowledge about what goes on in this school."

"I wonder how many of J's contacts are secretly

working with her," Hack mused. He took off his glasses and used them to scratch his head.

My stomach heaved. I had wanted to tell my friends about the key job, even if I couldn't include them in it. But I couldn't tell them I was working with the snitch Becca. In their minds, I'd be a traitor to rival Benedict Arnold and Darth Vader.

"Cricket might be," Case said. "He doesn't have anything to lose."

Cricket was a lanky guy who always wore a denim jacket, even in the summer. He was a professional informant; he knew everything that went on in the school, from honest business to under-the-table dealings. A good person to go to for a little extra information on a mark or a client. But he stayed honest. He might skulk a little, but he'd never do anything sketchy enough to attract Becca's attention. And although he knew about everyone else's closet skeletons, he had none of his own.

"Nothing to gain, either," Hack said. "He's just below her radar; he'll want to keep it that way. No, my guess is Tomboy Tate. You know how girls like to stick together." He put his glasses, with a fresh thumbprint, back on.

Case's jaw dropped. "Tomboy Tate's a girl?"

"Dude, you knew that!" I said.

"No, I didn't." Case pulled a pencil out of his pocket

and stuck it behind his ear. "She's *your* contact, J. I've only heard you talk about meeting 'Tate' for intel on your marks. I've never met her. And you call her Tomboy."

Hack laughed. "'Tomboy' means a girl, genius. And you've met her."

"When?"

"Back in February. Remember that snow day when a girl came over and told Jeremy the school's doors were only going to be unlocked for the next half hour, so if he had anything to retrieve, he'd better get moving?"

Case's eyes bugged. "*That* was Tate?"

"Yeah!"

"She's cute! I should . . . give her a call or something." Case nudged me. "What do you think?"

"About Tate? Go for it, but I'm warning you, the last guy who asked her out got punched in the stomach."

"Huh." Case frowned, then shook his head. "I'll be fine. No, I'm talking about the snitch. Do you think she's compromised some of your contacts?"

I faked a laugh. "If she had, I'd know."

"I suppose that's true. They'd have spontaneously grown devil horns." As I rubbed my forehead, feeling conspicuous, Case led us to homeroom. "She's an evil little—what the . . . ?"

A small crowd waited outside the door, made up of

our classmates in the sixth grade and a number of seventh graders. My stomach heaved again; I immediately regretted drinking orange juice with breakfast. Mark had already started.

Case and Hack, however, didn't know that. "Whose birthday is it?" Hack said, pushing past people. "I didn't know someone ordered a party."

Case nudged his way past too, keeping his gloved hands tucked against his chest.

As soon as I tried to pass, though, kids grabbed my elbows and I was blasted with noise as everyone talked over one another.

"My French book—"

"My sweatshirt—"

"My gym uniform—"

"Gone, just like that."

"Hey, people, leave him alone," Hack called, but they didn't hear him.

It took three whole minutes of waving my hands before I managed to calm everyone down. "Okay, listen to me." I pulled out a pencil and a sheet of notebook paper. "Pass this around. Write down your name and what was taken. Whoa, one at a time!" The paper circulated, crumpling in the crowd's haste to each be the next person served.

"What was that about?" Case asked after the crowd scattered.

I peeked around, acting like I was making sure I was out of Becca's or a teacher's earshot, while really trying to come up with a good excuse that didn't involve explaining my temporary alliance with the school's most notorious, possibly demonic detective. "What was what about?"

Okay, not my most clever response, but is lying to your friends ever easy?

"You never have this much business," Case said. "Especially this early in the day. What's going on?"

"Must be a crime wave or something. Don't worry; I'm on it." I smiled.

"This is bad," Hack said, taking the list. "I can't have a virus ready by second period, but I might be able to take control of Mr. Gumby's computer remotely. While he's dealing with it, you can sneak out and get a start tracking down all these things."

Case nodded. "I can run interference during third period. You can skip that too. Use your new hall pass. With lunch, that's three straight periods of free retrieval time."

I tried not to squirm as I remembered my promise to Becca not to retrieve anything but the key. I took the list from Hack and looked it over. "Thanks, guys, but not today. I don't even know who the thief is." Another lie from a lying liar who lies to his best friends.

"Are you sure?" Hack said. "This is just like that guy back in December. Thieves who go for quantity over quality—"

"Are going to sell everything, I know. And soon." My rib cage seemed to be shrinking and squeezing everything up my throat. "I'll stop the thief and get everything back. But right now, the best thing for me to do is analyze who was stolen from and where their lockers are. Look for a pattern. Okay?"

I looked Case in the eyes and refused to break first. Maintaining eye contact looks honest, hides a lie.

Case glanced away. "Okay." Then he frowned and scratched his head. Hack chewed his lip.

That trick about keeping eye contact when lying? Yeah, they know it too.

I smiled, but I felt like throwing up as I went inside the room and sat down. When all this was over, I'd make it up to them. I'd tell them everything. Well, almost everything. Becca would be too hard to explain.

THE REST OF THE DAY, THOUGH

busy, was normal until sixth period, the eighth grade's lunchtime. Becca had told me she could get me out of class so we could initiate phase one, but frankly, I didn't trust her to come through. So I was surprised when she showed up as I was figuring out the value of x, and more than a little annoyed when she began to talk.

"Principal McDuff sent me for . . . Jeremy Wilderson?" she asked, letting her voice jump up at the end like she didn't know who I was. Like anyone would buy that. "He wants to see him in his office right now."

The whispering started. Although no one openly discussed my work except in dire circumstances like this crime wave, most students knew what I did and what Becca did. This would hit the rumor mill as soon as class ended and students could text again. The troublemakers were already at it, their hands flying under the desks.

Ms. Manuel looked concerned. "What is this about?"

Becca shrugged and smiled. "I don't know; he wouldn't tell me. But he did say it might take a while."

Ms. Manuel turned to me. "Jeremy, take your backpack and go with Becca."

I did as she said while the whispering crescendoed behind me. ("Crescendoed" . . . like it? Music class.) I could feel my face turning red.

"What was that?" I asked as soon as Becca and I were alone in the halls. "Couldn't you have done anything— anything at all—to *not* make me look guilty?" With the rash of break-ins and my reputation, I wouldn't have been surprised if my math class had already decided to print up WANTED: JEREMY WILDERSON posters.

"You are guilty, Wilderson," Becca said. "Is it wrong of me to want the rest of the school to see that?"

"It is when it means we might not stop Mark. Or do you want him to get away?"

Becca sighed. "If I did, do you think I'd be working with you?"

"Point taken." But I still didn't trust her. While she spoke about the school's rule book like it had floated down to Scottsville on a golden cloud, she bent those rules when it suited her. For all I knew, she'd break her promise as soon as the key was back where it belonged.

"How long do we have?" Becca asked.

"I can crack his locker in ten minutes, and after that it's easy. You know what you have to do?"

"Do all your thieving partners need constant reminders on how to do their jobs?"

"Okay, no need to get snarky. Do whatever you want. Just keep him away for twenty minutes."

"Don't let the teachers catch you."

I put my hand on my heart. "Why, Miss Mills, I didn't know you cared."

She gave me an ice-cold death stare. "If you get caught, it makes me look bad because I got you out of class." Becca left toward the hall outside the cafeteria.

I shook my head and crept toward the eighth-grade hallway. Class hours aren't the best time to be working. Teachers do their rounds, kids go to the bathroom to ditch class and sometimes to actually use the bathroom, and once in a while classes get out early, all of which can be awkward when you're kneeling in front of a locker that isn't yours with your ear pressed against the metal.

I didn't see anyone as I walked down the eighth-grade hallway. I knew roughly where Mark's locker was from confronting him the day before, but I also may have dared Hack to pull up the list of student locker numbers during Mr. Gumby's third-period computer class. Mark's was 823.

Before beginning work on the locker, I closed my eyes and listened for footsteps, doors opening and closing, anything that might cause trouble. Nothing. Good.

Middle school lockers have a keyhole as well as the standard combination lock, for the infamous master key. I could have picked it, but my picks might have left marks on the keyhole, and with the master key being hot, I couldn't risk it. So I went for old-fashioned code-breaking.

I placed my ear against the locker door and spun the lock, listening for the sweet spot where the acoustics were just right to hear the contact points click.

All school combination locks have three numbers, making them three-wheel locks. To crack the lock, I'd need to line up the wheels just right, in the right order, to allow a metal bar called a fence to drop and open the lock. I parked the wheels at zero and slowly, carefully, spun the dial forward to the right, listening as the numbers passed one by one. My eyes were closed; anyone who wanted to sneak up on me would have the perfect chance to do it.

A click. A few numbers later, another. I kept turning until I heard the contact points click six times total, for the left and right of the three numbers. Every time it clicked, I opened my eyes and made a note of which number it landed on. Then I parked the wheels three before zero and did it again, counting the clicks and aligning the numbers.

This was going to take forever. After a few minutes, I had my numbers: seven, twelve, and forty-two. But in what order? The clicks couldn't tell me that; they just let me know where the notches on the wheels were. I'd blown through too much time; I still needed to search the locker before Becca came back. How long did I have? Ten minutes? Five?

I entered the numbers in the order I found them and pulled on the door. No go. I tried them backward and still didn't get it. How many other combinations were there? I didn't have time to try them all out.

Fine. If I couldn't manipulate the lock, I might still manipulate the safe. Most Scottsville Middle lockers had a trick, and I knew it. I hoped Mark's wasn't an exception. I pounded the top corners of the door and kicked the latch beside the lock. The door swung open with a clang and a red water balloon catapulted at my face.

"Whoa! What the . . . ?"

Although my head dodged, my hand sprung to action. Moving like a video game character, I reached for the balloon as it passed my face, scooped it out of the air before it could hit the floor, then cushioned the impact by dropping my hand for a short distance with the projectile.

Saved. My hand hung inches from the hard floor, which would likely have broken the tight skin of the balloon and splattered liquid all over me and the hall, leaving puddles of proof that someone had broken into the locker.

I lifted the balloon to eye level and examined it. The liquid inside wasn't water; it was too thick. Paint, maybe? Good thing Rick and I were the annual champs of the Wilderson Fourth of July Family Picnic water-balloon toss.

The inside of the locker held the catapult rig, a cardboard contraption connected to the locker door by a string. When the door opened, the catapult would fire at whoever stood there. Did I mention the trap was rigged so it would work best on a very short person?

"Clever, Mark," I muttered. "But no cigar."

I have no idea what that expression means either.

I admit, I felt a little giddy at that point. I had cracked the locker—in record time, I might add—and dodged a trap that would have marked me as a locker-breaking thief for all the teachers to see. I was flying high.

So, of course, that would be the moment I heard footsteps from around the corner.

My heart kicked my lungs, but I calmed myself down. The steps were far away; I could still do this.

Putting the water balloon beside the catapult, I started with Mark's jacket, pulling out the pockets as fast as I could. Nothing. I even felt the lining to see if the creep had sewn the key there for safekeeping. Which, in hindsight, doesn't make sense. Trapped in a lining, the key would be too hard to access.

At the bottom of the locker, books and papers were stacked haphazardly. I pushed through them, leaning them up against the side as I went. I even flipped through the pages of the books. Nothing. Nada. Zip.

The footsteps rounded the corner, and I froze. A girl, an eighth grader I'd never worked for or against, ignored me as she went to the water fountain beside the girls' bathroom across the hall from Mark's locker, drank, and left. I sighed. I had a little more time.

Mark wasn't the kind of guy to have little baskets stuck to his door, so that left the cubby at the top of the locker, where the catapult and water balloon lay. I pushed the trap aside and examined the back, finding some pens, old erasers, and cough drops. Nothing big enough to hide a key in or under. I pushed them around anyway.

My hand caught paper, and I paused. It was the twenty-dollar bill Mark had tried to pay me with. "Well, well, well."

I was angry. Mark had used me, set me up to take his fall, forced me to work with Becca, and tried to splatter me with paint. This wasn't about money for me, and I wanted Mark to know it. Using one of Mark's pens, I wrote with my left hand under Andrew Jackson's face, *You can't buy skill.* I reread it. Good. Mark would know who wrote it, but teachers couldn't link those words to me. It was all about proof, who had it and who didn't.

Speaking of which, I had to reset the trap. Couldn't let Mark prove I'd been there, could I? I readjusted the arm of the catapult and nested the water balloon in the cup. When I drew back my hand, it was stained with red.

Oh, perfect. Looking closer at the balloon, I noticed a slow dribble of red paint from the loose end, where the rubber was knotted. That explained why it hadn't burst. It must have been punctured when I caught it or when I pushed it aside to search the locker. If it had been water, it would have sprayed everywhere, but the thick paint just bubbled out. My stomach lurched as I thought about how much trouble I'd almost been in.

I should have been more careful and treated the balloon like the live grenade it was. The red paint coated my palm, smearing with every movement. I'd have to be careful to reset the string without getting paint on it—

Footsteps down the hall, around the corner. Voices echoed. Mark and Becca!

"I appreciate this," Mark said. "With all the thefts, I'm glad you're coming with me to check on my locker."

"No problem," Becca said, smirking. I didn't know a smirk could be audible. "Maybe we'll find some evidence."

Dang! Double dang! That was the last time I'd tell Becca Mills to "do whatever you want." Forget resetting the trap. I closed the locker door with my elbow and looked for a place to hide. I had only seconds.

The girls' bathroom across the hall. It was my one option. I'd just have to hope that no one was inside.

I made the door with less than a second to spare. No one was inside, thank goodness. I looked around. "Wow. It's really clean in here."

I could hear them through the door. "Looks like nothing's wrong," Becca said, her voice calm. "No signs of forced entry."

"A thief might not need to force his entry," Mark said. "Let me look inside. Stand back."

I heard the locker door open. "Someone was in here," Mark said.

"Really? How can you tell?"

Becca sounded so cool and disinterested, so different from how she spoke to me. Was this what she sounded like most of the time? I thought her voice was permanently set on either brownnosing (for teachers) or simmering with acidic hate (for me).

"Look. The balloon's broken. There's paint all over my catapult. It wasn't like that when I left it."

"Well, balloons do that, especially the cheap kind," Becca said. "At my friend Elena's birthday party, half the balloons exploded before we took them out of the cooler. Do you have any incontrovertible evidence for me?"

Incontrovertible. Good word. I'd have to remember that one. And it sounded like I'd done a good job covering my tracks. I fist-pumped, which spread the paint from my palm to my fingers. Great.

"Everything's been moved around."

"It looks neat to me," Becca said.

"Exactly. My locker wasn't this neat last I saw it. And he went through my jacket. All the pockets are turned out. He can't have gotten far. We should go after him."

My heart fluttered. Would he come looking for me? I couldn't let him catch me hiding in a girls' bathroom!

"Hang on," Becca said. "Our not-so-bright thief left us a lot of evidence when he straightened up your locker. Let's make a case, and then we'll get him." The smugness in her voice made me grit my teeth. "Has anything been taken?"

After a few seconds of silence Mark spoke. "No, nothing's missing. But wait. I swear there wasn't anything written on this when I saw it last." He'd found the twenty-dollar bill.

"Really?" A pause. I pictured Becca clenching her fists. "Why the money?"

"What?"

"It's odd, that's all."

"Why?"

"Because I see a stack of notebooks here, all full of paper. Why leave a note on a twenty-dollar bill hidden at the back of a locker? Did the money have some kind of meaning, some significance?"

I smiled. When I'd told Becca everything, I'd told her *everything*. She knew all about Mark trying to pay me. She knew the answer to the question. It made me wonder how much she already knew when she asked *me* questions.

"No," Mark answered. After a pause he added, "I guess the thief didn't want to rip out any pages."

"Well, the good news is you can still spend the money, even if it's been written on. Why don't you go back to lunch and I'll do some forensics here? We'll catch this thief. By the way, do you have any idea who did this?"

Mark snorted. "You know who it is."

"Right. Wilderson. He's gone too far this time. Now, I wasn't kidding about you going back to lunch. I need an untouched crime scene."

One pair of feet walked away, down the hall. I still had my ear against the door when it jerked open and Becca walked in with a dangerous smile on her little face. "Fancy meeting you here. Oh," she said, looking at my paint-stained hand. "Looks like I caught you red-handed."

"That was a really bad pun," I said as I walked over to a sink. "Now I hurt inside."

"I know, but I couldn't pass up the opportunity." She stood there, watching, as I struggled to turn the hot-water spigot, which must have rusted to the sink. When I finally succeeded and started washing the paint off, she coughed. Twice.

"What?"

"You do know this is the girls' room."

"I'm aware of that. How did you know I'd be in here?"

"I heard your footsteps. You didn't move for long, so I knew you weren't far. And this is the only hiding place, unless you'd shoved yourself into a locker." She smiled and pulled her camera out of her pocket. "Jeremy Wilderson, lurking in a ladies' room. Say 'cheese.'" She snapped a picture of me at the sink, unable to dodge or hide my face. "I think I'll print a copy of this one."

I felt like I was at war and losing. Bad. "Can't we just congratulate ourselves on a job well done and let bygones be bygones?"

"The note on the money. Don't you think that was a bit much?"

"I thought it would help sell the con."

At the word "con," Becca flinched.

"That came very close to leaving enough evidence to indict yourself."

"I never leave evidence unless I want to. You know that." I scrubbed harder at my hand, but the paint didn't come off. "I'm so glad I didn't get this all over my face. I'd look like the cafeteria's red Jell-O salad."

"You wouldn't have lost much. But here." Becca turned up the hot water on my hand. Taking a handful of paper towels, she pumped enough soap over them to wash a Chevy pickup. Then she grabbed my wet wrist.

"What are you doing?" I tried to pull away, but she didn't let go.

Becca rolled her eyes. "You're never going to get it off at that rate. I can't afford to have anyone see that paint and link you to Mark's locker and suspect that you're working with me. I don't think you understand how much I'm risking. If anyone knew I teamed with you on this case, it would destroy any faith people have in me. And I don't just mean kids. Teachers, too."

Really? She was giving me a lecture on risk when I was hiding in a girls' bathroom and set up by a crime-lord wannabe to take the fall for a series of thefts?

"Are you sure this isn't just an excuse to hold my hand?"

Becca responded by grating the soapy paper down my stained hand, removing a lot of paint by scraping off my top layer of skin.

"Oww."

"Did that feel like a love note to you?"

"Well, you are hiding evidence for me. If that's not true love, I don't know what is."

"I'm not going to dignify that with a response." Becca bit her lip. "I thought you would have taken that money instead of written on it. Since it was supposed to be your payment and all."

"You made it clear that I'm not allowed to retrieve anything on pain of getting turned in, not as long as we work together. And, oh yeah, I'm not a thief."

"Liar." Becca's hand clenched, cutting off the flow of blood to my wrist. As I squirmed, she said, "You have a long history of thefts, Wilderson. The longer I work with you, the closer I come to finding what I need to prove what you are. Why don't you just confess and save us both the trouble?"

I twisted my hand free from Becca's grip. "We both know you have nothing without my official confession. Maybe that would be different if you knew how to do your job right."

"I know how to do my job."

"You were supposed to keep Mark away by any means necessary. For twenty minutes. I had maybe fifteen before I had to run for it." I examined my hand. The paint was gone, but the skin burned. What do they put in that soap?

Becca threw the wad of soapy paper towels at my face. "Well, excuse me," she said as I fumbled the dripping mess. "Mark was pretty determined, and I couldn't make it obvious I was keeping him from his locker. I have a reputation at this school."

"Yeah, well, so do I. It would be great if you could respect that."

She laughed. "Respect? That will happen on the far side of never."

I gritted my teeth. What was it about this girl that made me want to argue until the zombie apocalypse had come and gone? *Remember the plan. Remember Mark and all those kids whose stuff has been stolen.* "Can you come over after school today? There are some phase-two details I want to hammer out."

"No, you'd better come to my house," Becca said. "My parents won't be home, and I'm an only child. It will be more secret."

"Asking me over. Bold move, considering this is only our second date."

"You wish."

"Not really."

A girl with curly blond hair walked into the bathroom and turned red when she saw me. I grinned and waved as I walked past her. "It's all yours," I said.

Finally I got the last word over Becca. And it felt so sweet.

MINE MAY NOT BE THE MOST

reputable line of work, but I keep my promises. After Mom drove me home from school, I made sure no one was watching before walking across the street to Becca's house. Hey, I have a reputation to uphold.

When Becca opened the door, she said, "Don't thieves prefer coming in through the window?"

"The amateurs, maybe. The good ones walk through the front door. Shouldn't you know that?"

"I'm not a thief."

"What a coincidence! Me neither."

"Good, because if you do anything that even looks like thieving for the rest of this case, that's it. I will haul you and all the evidence I have on you down to Principal McDuff, and you will take the fall for this. I'll deal with Mark on my own. Got it?"

"What evidence?"

"That's my business. But I'll have enough to make my threats stick."

"Got it." I thought about all those kids with missing stuff and wished I could do something to help them instead of being stuck obeying a bunch of stupid rules laid on me by the school detective.

"Promise," she said.

"Cross my heart and hope to die."

"Not your heart. I'm not sure you have one. Cross those sticky little fingers you love so much." Becca grabbed my arm. "Come in; we have a lot to talk about."

I followed her inside to her kitchen table, where we'd first struck our deal. In the center of the table a plate of cookies, two glasses, and a gallon of milk waited.

I froze. "What is that?" I asked, pointing at the spread.

"Snacks," Becca said. "Enjoy them while you can; I think prison's sugar-free."

"What did you do to them? Did you bake truth serum into the cookies? Is it in the milk?"

Becca rolled her eyes. She did that often. "We have a lot to plan, and I thought we'd want something to eat. And if you'd like to meet the devious, truth-serum-lacing chef, look right over there." She pointed to a garbage can where an empty store-bought cookie package lay crumpled.

"If it's safe, *you* eat one." I knew she hadn't laced the cookies with anything. She wasn't that high-tech. I just enjoyed bugging her about it too much.

"Oh, come on," Becca groaned. But she took a cookie and shoved it in her mouth.

After making a big show of examining the chocolate chips and sniffing the cookies, I did the same.

"Sit down," Becca said, gesturing to a chair.

"Are you going to push me over again?"

"Depends. Are you going to ask for it again?"

I looked at her but pulled the chair out and sat down, keeping the chair's legs planted on the floor.

"So, phase one went pretty well," Becca said.

"I guess," I replied, tucking my hands in my lap. "At least I didn't get caught."

"Did you find the key?"

"Trust me—"

"I never trust you, Wilderson."

"Will you let me finish my sentence? I was going to say, 'Trust me, you would know if I found the key.' You'd have it in your hand. Because I'm honest."

"Yeah. And I just made a down payment on the Taj Mahal. How do I know you wouldn't lie and keep the master key if you found it?"

"If that were the case, you'd know I had the key

because I wouldn't be here eating processed cookie. I'd be breaking into your locker."

Becca grinned. "Was that a confession I heard?"

"No."

"Are you sure? It sounded like you admitted to wanting to break into my locker."

"That's not what I said, and it's not a confession."

She shrugged. "Why don't we just listen again and check. . . ." Her eyes widened as she dug in her empty pocket.

I casually held up the camera. "Looking for this?" Even when hidden in a pocket, a camera capable of filming makes a decent tape recorder.

"You little *thief*."

"Hey, I never intended to remove it from the premises. This is more of a relocation. Don't worry; I turned it off when I found it."

"And when would that be?"

"When you pulled me inside. Here, you can have it back." I slid it across the table. "The battery, though, will be returned when I leave."

I thought Becca would strangle me. "How dare you pick my pocket!"

"How dare you try to record me when we're working together? We have to be able to trust each other, or this will never work." I sighed. "Just for now, I have to know you're not trying to trap me."

"And I have to know you aren't going to be a thief every opportunity you get."

"I've followed your rules. I think I've earned the right to establish one of my own."

Becca picked up the camera and popped the back off. She shook her head at the missing battery. But then she smiled. "I have to say, I'm impressed."

"Have to do better than that to trick me. Mark learned that today. Does that mean you won't try to catch me in a recorded confession?"

"Okay. But just until we have the key. After that, you're fair game."

"Good." Enough of this. The faster we got through our meeting, the sooner I could get out of here. Despite the camera, the cookies and milk made our planning session feel too much like a friendly get-together, and that was a dangerous illusion. It was like believing a king cobra was a shoelace.

"Speaking of Mark," I said, "how did things go on your end? What did you find?"

Becca laid the camera on the table. "I found evidence that a short thief with red paint on his hands rifled through Mark's stuff."

I clenched my fists. "*I'm* short? Pot, meet kettle."

"Don't be so sensitive. The path to inner peace begins with accepting your flaws." Becca's face lost its superiority and she added, "You were listening to us, right?"

I nodded.

"Did you like how Mark wouldn't tell me why the twenty was important? But he knows it was you who wrote on it."

"Great." I poured a glass of milk and took a swig. "Now, phase two. I can get in, no problem, but you need to keep the mark busy while I do my thing."

"He's not a movie star, Wilderson. You don't have to give him a title."

"What?"

"His name is Mark. You don't have to call him *the* Mark."

It took a moment to register, but then it clicked and I burst out laughing. "Oh, gosh, no," I said when I had calmed down. "But it is funny that his name is . . ." I lost it again.

Becca was not even sort of as amused as I was. "Tell me what you know."

The way her fingers gripped the surface of the table made me choke back my laughter. "The 'mark' is the target. The person you're trying to take down. In this case, his name is also Mark. So Mark's the mark." I stifled a giggle.

What? It's funny!

"Oh. Thief jargon," Becca said, relaxing. "I'm not fluent in that language."

"I'm sorry. I suppose I should call him the perk so as not to offend you."

It was Becca's turn to laugh. "It's 'perp,' thief boy. As in, 'That perp Jeremy Wilderson really got paint on his hands when he was knocking over Mark's locker.'"

I smirked. "'Knocking over'? What was that about not speaking thief language?"

Becca smirked. "I said I wasn't fluent in it. I never said I couldn't manage a phrase or two."

That made us both laugh. But then, a moment later, we sat silent and awkward, sipping our milk. For a second there it had been almost like we were friends. Like she wasn't out to get me.

She must have felt the weirdness, because Becca closed her eyes, and when she opened them, the icy hardness had returned. "Okay, Wilderson. I have some things to talk to you about regarding phase two. I've been thinking about it, and I've noticed the potential for a . . . mishap."

"Like today's mishap, which wouldn't have happened

if someone hadn't brought the perp/mark over too early. Did you do that on purpose to catch me in the act?"

Becca ignored the question. "I need you to pay attention to what I'm about to say. We've got Mark scared."

"Good."

"But that means that he's not going to leave his backpack unattended. I know you wanted to search it while he's in gym class, but for the first time in your life, be honest: Do you think Mark's going to leave anything of his where you could search it?"

I sipped my milk. "If it were me, I wouldn't."

"That's what I thought."

I leaned forward. "Then what do you suggest? Gym class is the best chance I have of getting to his backpack. It's the only time you're required to leave your stuff behind in an empty room, and backpacks are never locked up." Though, technically, Mark could bring the bag into the gym and keep it on the sidelines. I wouldn't put it past him.

Becca ran her finger down her glass. "We could call him out of class for something. Like what I did with you. I'd have a reason. I could talk to him as a peer mentor about his troubles with you."

"Good idea. It would work, except that he could still bring his backpack with him. Even if he, by some miracle, left it behind, I still couldn't get to it while it was sitting in the middle of a busy classroom."

Becca looked up. "It's the best idea we have. Unless you want to try gym class."

"Gym class may work better. Or maybe in the lunch-room." If only we had a scheduled reason for Mark to leave his backpack behind, like a field trip or an assembly or a—

Fire drill.

I couldn't believe I hadn't thought of it before. During a fire drill, students had to leave their stuff inside. Teachers were militant about it. Mark would have no choice but to abandon his bag.

"What?" Becca asked. "You look like you just had an idea."

"Yeah." I had an idea, one that was so dangerous and stupid and lawbreaking I knew I could never tell Becca. "I think I may be able to manage getting to the backpack while he's in class."

"Really?" Becca raised an eyebrow. "All eyes will be on you."

"It's not ideal. But I have some favors to call in, and I think I can make this work."

"Eighth-grade lunch is two periods after ours. He'll be in class while you're at lunch."

"I can work with that."

"What are the details?"

"Haven't hammered them out yet. It may end up being kind of spur-of-the-moment. Leave this part of it to me."

Becca frowned. "You *will* tell me what you're doing, like we agreed, right?"

"Absolutely." Absolutely *not*. The plan only worked if we separated Mark from his backpack, and the only way to do that was to have a fire drill.

The good news was I could schedule the fire drill myself. The bad news was, if I got caught, I would be in more trouble than I'd ever been in before.

"Keep me posted. On everything." Becca smiled. "And phase two is a go."

"Great. Well, if that's it, I'll be on my way." I stood, ready to make my exit, but Becca motioned for me to sit.

"Not yet. Right now I need to teach you how to look for evidence."

I sank into the chair. "Why?"

"In case you need it. If you get caught, I get in trouble, so I need you to not get caught. This will speed up your search time." She pushed a sheet of paper across the table. "This is a picture of a fake crime scene. Tell me what you see."

I could keep telling you how our meeting went, but after that it got long and boring and Becca made me jump through all these hoops to get ready for phase two. I left feeling brain-dead, excited, and terrified. After all, I'd never "scheduled" a fire drill before. The game had escalated. Let's hope I could escalate along with it.

FRIDAYS AT SCOTTSVILLE ARE

always kind of insane, but that Friday was worse than the grand opening of a devil's-food-cake stand at a chocoholics' convention.

When I got to school, buzzing with adrenaline over my unsavory plans for phase two, and went to get my books for class, they weren't there. None of them. Everything—my textbooks, notebooks, pens, highlighters—was gone. All I found was a piece of lined paper with a big winky face taped to the inside of my locker door. Under it was written, *Who said anything about buying?*

I crumpled up the piece of paper and crushed it to the bottom of my backpack. "Oh, it's on."

Maybe I could put my stuff in Case's or Hack's locker. At least I still had the books and notebooks I'd needed for homework the night before.

Outside homeroom, once again a huge crowd of clients waited for me. All of them had had things stolen, valuable things, from their lockers. My only consolation was that I was sure Becca, as the school's private investigator, had her own mob to deal with. I hoped she was blowing them off like I had to.

Again I had them all write their names and stolen property on a piece of paper and waved them on their way. That should have been the end of it, but then Case and Hack appeared. They weren't smiling.

"I'm glad to see you guys. Do you think I can put my stuff with yours? My locker's not safe right now."

"Since when are you afraid of a thief?" Case twirled a paintbrush, and Hack fidgeted with his glasses and hair and shirt.

"I'm not. Something's up with you. What happened?"

Case took a deep breath and placed the brush over his ear. "Our lockers aren't safe either. My locker was broken into. They took my new batch of hall passes."

"They got my tablet, too." Hack looked at me and shrugged. "Well, it's my mom's. But I need it back before she realizes I borrowed it."

I couldn't believe it. Mark couldn't just attack me directly; he had to go after my best friends, too. I was going to make him *hurt*.

My fingers itched. I wanted to ditch all my classes and track down Mark's stash, get back my books, Case's hall passes, and Hack's mom's tablet. Mark had to be keeping them somewhere nearby until he could get them out of the building. It would be so easy for me to find the loot and pay Mark back.

But if I did, Becca would find out. She's the best detective in school. Sure, she didn't have any evidence on me yet, but that could change in a heartbeat. If I ditched phase two to find my friends' stuff, I'd lose my chance to search Mark's bag and I'd have nothing to give Becca. She'd want to know why, and then she'd get mad. That could be the tipping point that would let her find enough to turn me in. A student's testimony, a teacher's comment that I missed class two days in a row . . . it could accumulate. Then Mark would maybe never go down for what he did and Case's and Hack's things would never turn up. Hack's mom would kill him for taking technology he wasn't allowed to have, again.

So all I could do was hand the list of stolen goods to Case and say, "Write down what was stolen and when."

Case took the paper. "You can't remember on your own?"

"It's not like that. I've got a lot to deal with. I don't want to count on remembering and then miss something.

I'll get your hall passes back. And Hack's mom's tablet. I promise."

"Sure you will." Case passed back the paper without writing on it and gave me an odd look.

"What was that?"

"What was what?"

I pointed at his face. "That look. Maybe all the new clients have got me unhinged, but I could have sworn you squinted at me. Like you were suspicious."

"Me? Suspicious of you, J? That's ridiculous." Case, while a master forger, is a terrible liar. It was like someone had taken his precious paints and the brush from his ear and stroked *I DON'T TRUST YOU* across his face.

"We're friends, Case. You can tell me anything. What's going on?"

"If we're friends, why won't you tell *us* what's going on?"

I should have expected them to confront me. I did; I'd just hoped it would happen later. "What?"

"We're not stupid. We know something big's happening and you're right in the middle of it. With a crime wave like this, you'd have to be." Case shook his head. "But you're not saying anything to us. You always tell us about your jobs, even the small ones. Why are you silent now? And you're not doing what you'd normally do. You're not acting like yourself. The J I know would already have retrieved most, if not all, of the stolen items. He wouldn't let people get ripped off like this, making a list instead of acting."

"If you're so worried, *you* go retrieve it all."

"That's not my area. I'd get caught like that." Case snapped his fingers. "You're the sneaky one. Like the thief responsible for this crime wave, you can get in and out of a locker without leaving clues behind. Come to think of it, you're also acting so distant, like you have something to hide."

"Whoa." I raised my hands. "Maybe I'm hallucinating, but it sounded like you just insinuated that *I'm* the one out robbing lockers."

"We don't believe that," Case said. "Really, we don't."

"Yeah? Because it sounds like an accusation to me." I looked at my friends and the distrust on their faces. "We made a *pact*, guys, to never use our skills for evil. I'd never break that. You should know that."

"Calm down, J! We know." Hack squirmed more, looking like he'd rather be sitting in front of the principal, trying to explain how he cracked the school's firewalls again, than be with us. "It's not us. It's other people."

I froze. "What do you mean?"

Case shrugged. "People are starting to talk. They're saying no one benefits as much from this crime wave as you."

"That's insane."

"Maybe, but what they're saying is making a lot of sense. Hear me out. With every locker knocked over, your client list grows. Some people on the bus this morning commented how easy it would be for you to return their stuff if you were the one who'd had it all along. When you help your clients, they talk you up. They recommend you to their friends. You become a legend, just like you want. Everyone will remember the guy who stopped the biggest crime wave Scottsville ever had. Even being the thief behind the crime wave is its own legacy."

"I'm not stealing anything!"

"I know. We both know," Case said, hands raised in a calming gesture. "So do other people, but the problem is, they're speculating now. If it's hitting the rumor mill, how long before the snitch picks up on it?"

"Since when do you care what Becca would think?" I took a deep breath, trying not to blow up. "If I'm the thief, why would I steal from you? You're my friends."

Case shrugged. "So we wouldn't suspect you. Because those passes and the tablet are valuable. Because it would look good if you went out to 'avenge' your friends."

I rubbed the space between my eyebrows. "Oh, boy." If people were already starting to talk, then I was in trouble. "What did you guys say?"

"We had your back," Hack said. "We told them you'd never steal *from* them, only *for* them. It's just a few people who enjoy watching a hero turn dirty and fall from grace. No one important. But we can't defend you as much as we want because we don't know anything."

"J," Case said, "tell us what you're doing. We can help you if we know what your plan is to catch the thief."

"You know what I know." A lie.

Case pointed at my face. "You're hiding something. I can see it when you lie to us. I know you're busy. I know you're working *something*. You always are. Yesterday I went to your house to talk about the crime wave, and you weren't home. You're always home after school in case someone comes over with a job."

"No one told me you came over," I said.

"Rick answered the door."

"Oh. That explains it."

"So, where were you?" Case asked.

This was the moment of truth. Literally. What was I doing? These were my friends. They'd had my back hundreds of times, on hundreds of jobs. If I couldn't trust them, I couldn't trust anyone. I could tell them the truth, about Mark and the key and my involvement and working with—working with B—

I chickened out. "I was looking into the locker thefts."

"Then why doesn't it look like you're doing anything about it?" Case waved at the list in my hand.

"It's not that simple this time. Scottsville has never had a crime wave like this. I can't treat it like my usual jobs." I felt like I'd eaten a burger and discovered it was made of leftover mystery meat. I hated lying to my friends and hiding my work from them. But it was for the best. "This job is different. It's dangerous."

"So bring us in on it," Hack said. "We can help you if you'd just let us."

Oh yeah, and Case and Hack and I could all sit around at Becca Mills's table, eating cookies and drinking milk. That would go over well. "I can't," I said. "I'm sorry."

Case gritted his teeth. "Why not?"

"Because it's not safe."

Hack took off his glasses and used them to scratch his head. "For you? Or for us? We can take care of ourselves."

"We're not babies," Case said. "We don't need you to protect us from the big, bad world. We can help."

"Not with this one. Not this time."

"You know what? Fine." Case jabbed a finger at me. "Go it alone. Sorry we're too pathetic or too untrustworthy for you to confide in when your job gets dangerous. I hope whoever you're talking to cares enough to keep you from self-destructing."

"I'm not talking to anyone else." A lie, but Becca's name could not come up.

"Aren't you? This job is too big for one person. If you're not confiding in us, then you're working with someone else. Someone that you trust more than your friends."

"I trust you."

"If you did, you'd talk to us. Unless everyone else is right and you *are* the thief behind the crime spree."

I froze, stung. "I know you don't believe that."

"Maybe I do, maybe I don't. But maybe I don't *trust* you enough to tell you what I think." Case clenched his fists, making his gloves bunch up.

I was shaking. "That's great. Just wonderful. Maybe we shouldn't tell each other anything at all."

Hack shook his head. "Don't be like that, J—"

Case stopped him with a wave. "If you get into trouble, don't come running to us."

"I won't. Enjoy homeroom." I turned to leave. "I've got a lot of work to do."

No one followed me to the boys' bathroom, where I found an empty stall and seethed.

Some friends I had. How could Case and Hack get so angry when all I wanted to do was protect them from Mark and Becca? Couldn't they trust my judgment after all we'd been through?

As angry as I was at my so-called friends, I was livid with Mark. Mark was going to *pay* for what he had done to my life. And soon. That eighth grader was lucky it was almost the weekend; he would not get another day to steal from innocent people. Not when I, with Becca's help, could stop him.

My enemy was my only ally, and my friends were upset with me. How did this happen?

I kicked the stall door, slamming it against the frame. Then I pulled a notebook out of my backpack and penned a couple of notes to Tomboy Tate and Cricket. Becca had said no retrieving, but I didn't care. Before school ended, I had an important job to do. There were a couple of things I needed to get back before Mark had any kind of chance to sell them or lose them. The stakes were high, but it didn't matter. I had to make things right.

I SKIPPED HOMEROOM, BUT

I couldn't stay hidden for long or the teachers would get suspicious. I stashed my backpack up in the bathroom's ceiling tiles and then used my fake hall pass to find Tate and give her my note. By the time the bell rang for first period, everything was ready to go and I had reentered the flow of the school day.

My anger at Mark and guilt/annoyance with Case and Hack dissolved, for a while, under the craziness of the rest of my day. People kept coming up to me—with no regard for who might be nearby listening or the air of mystery I try to keep—telling me what items had vanished from their sealed lockers. Could I, pretty please, find it for them?

On top of that I saw Mark watching me as I walked from third to fourth period. A couple of the muscular guys who had pushed him into the lockers the other day were laughing and slapping his back like a friend, which worried me. Mark had gotten street cred since the last time we met. When he saw me looking, he smiled and hoisted his red backpack higher onto his shoulder. Who carries his backpack from class to class in *middle school*? I'll tell you who: someone who has something to hide.

Mark knew I'd broken into his locker. Writing on the twenty dollars would have made that undeniable. *Good,* I thought. I wanted him to know it was me who'd bring him down. He needed to know that he couldn't toy with Jeremy Wilderson, retrieval specialist, without swift and ruthless comeuppance.

But my blood still ran cold when I saw him. Mark was smart enough to play me and becoming better connected every day. If he wanted to, he could get one of his new friends to attack me after school and I wouldn't see it coming. That was why I needed to keep Case and Hack out of this job, and what Becca was for, if I could trust her enough to have my back. And if she didn't catch me in my . . . extracurricular activities.

I was grateful for lunchtime when it came. At least until the "fire drill," it would be quieter than the rest of my day; I didn't think there was anyone else left in the school to hire me. Also, I wouldn't be sitting with Case and Hack.

Sitting alone at one of the tables too close to the teachers to be fun, I watched my best friends talk and eat. I knew what they were saying. They were debating whether I didn't trust them enough to count on them or if it really was that dangerous a job. But sooner or later Hack would mention how his mom was thinking about shortening his sentence because of good behavior, and then Case would say that meant Hack was free to come to the county's summer art competition—Case would mention it; he seemed to manage to work that competition and his entry into every casual conversation lately. I'd sat through many of his tangents on the tiny mistakes he might have made in color choice and detailing, but how it should be okay because his competitors were "mouth-breathing troglodytes."

That's Case for you.

I bit my lip, which tasted like weak cheese sauce. Part of me wanted to go over and explain everything. If I made it clear that they couldn't get involved, I could tell them what I was doing. I could outline for them my plan for getting back their stuff.

But the rest of me couldn't forget that as soon as trouble—real trouble—popped up, they'd decided I didn't trust them enough. Some friends. They'd feel so stupid once Mark got caught and they saw what I was really doing.

A crumpled piece of paper landed in my overcooked broccoli. I scooped it up and unfolded it under the table. It was from Becca.

Mark is in position. Phase two is a go.

"Great," I muttered. I wasn't looking forward to what I needed to do to make phase two happen; kids got arrested for faking a fire. Also, dodging Becca was going to be nerve-racking and awful. But it was our only chance, and I needed to work, to get my mind off Case and Hack. Plus, getting the chance to swat Mark around, metaphorically speaking, could only brighten my day.

After making sure I had the gear I needed for this job, I walked out of the cafeteria, once more "forgetting" to sign out. Once out the door, I peeked over my shoulder. Case and Hack were watching me. Case stood up.

"Oh, perfect." I hurried away before they could gain on me.

Ten minutes later, when I met her in the hall, Becca glared at me. "Where were you?"

"My friends are getting a little too curious. They tried to tail me when I left the cafeteria. I had to take the long way and pass through the gym before I lost them."

"That's the rub, isn't it? As soon as you go straight, your criminal friends get upset with you," Becca said. She turned and started walking down the hall.

"I never said they were upset."

"You didn't have to. Your face is redder than usual, and you wouldn't have even brought up your friends if they weren't a problem. I am the *snitch*, after all." She smiled, making me wonder how much else she knew. "What's the matter? Are they mad that you didn't cut them in on the take?"

"Ah, you've been studying thief language," I said. "As much as I would love to talk to you about my personal life and my friends—who have done nothing, by the way, and are none of your business—we have a job to do. Where's Mark now?"

Becca pointed to a door decorated with paper ducks and math symbols (I didn't get it either). "In that classroom. Now do your stuff."

"Sure. As soon as you leave."

Becca folded her arms. "I'm not leaving you alone."

"You'll have to. Mark is scared. He's running. If he sees you and me together, he could suspect you. We'd lose our edge."

She didn't look convinced. "I'll tell you everything," I said. "After it's over."

Becca nodded. "Okay. I'll trust you. This once. Partly because I think you have no plan and are making this up as you go, but mostly because if you go rogue I have a long list of things I can tell the principal."

Oh, *perfect*. "Just get out of here. Leave me to my part of this. And you better not be taping this."

"Of course not. I trust you, remember? You'd better not betray that trust." With that veiled threat, she left me to my illegal activities.

For illegal they were. I'm sure by now you're wondering what I was thinking, going to such lengths to stop Mark. Well, a true artist is completely devoted to his craft, and I was. I did everything it took to complete a job. Also, I was responsible for the key's theft, so I had to get it back, which meant making opportunities if they didn't come served up on a scratched plastic lunch tray.

Once Becca was gone, I looked around the hall and located the nearest fire alarm. Then I searched the ceiling for the bubbly CCTV cameras. One had a perfect view of the fire alarm—camera 15. I walked past it into the nearest *boys'* bathroom and waited, peering out the door to the hallway.

What I wasn't supposed to know, but had learned from long afternoons waiting for my mom to finish red-inking papers so we could go home, was that the cameras were linked to TVs in the office, watched by security guards and off-duty teachers. The feeds from the cameras rotated, showing a minute of footage before moving to the next camera. A careful person could figure out the cameras' schedule and know which ones were playing at Office Theater at which times. And I am a very careful person.

As I watched the digital wall clock, waiting for the minute to change, I took a small roll of duct tape (the kind they sell at hiking stores) out of my pocket and tore a strip off. I stuck the strip to the back of my hand just as the clock changed. In the office the camera feed jumped off camera 15 and on to camera 16. I only had a minute or two, so I raced to the fire alarm. A thrill of excitement charged through my arm as I reached out, gripped the handle, and pulled. I jumped out of the way as soon as the handle was down; some schools have fire alarms that spray the puller with ink.

Nothing happened, and thank goodness. I don't think I could have handled being attacked with paint two days in a row.

No, the alarm did nothing more than let out a very satisfying squeal. As scared I was of getting caught, the fear melted under a wave of exhilaration. Who hasn't dreamed of pulling the fire alarm?

As white lights flashed in the halls and the alarm blared, I pressed my back into the wall just outside Mark's math classroom, where the door would swing out. When it did swing out, the class hurrying away, I grabbed it, just long enough to transfer the tape to the door, right over the locking mechanism. (I'd learned that trick in social studies, when we studied the Watergate scandal).

Then I melted back into the crowd of classes hurrying outside and ducked back into the boys' bathroom to wait out the crowd. I entered a stall, remembering to leave the door slightly open, and sat on the toilet with my feet up. A few minutes later a teacher came in.

"Anyone in here?"

I didn't answer.

A few seconds passed and the teacher left. I waited a couple more minutes and crept out of the bathroom.

The hall was deserted; everyone was outside, getting counted to make sure no one was trapped inside by the nonexistent flames. I hoped that because I was supposed to be at lunch when the alarm went off, the teachers wouldn't notice my name was missing for enough time for me to do my job. I would come out later and join the students, making sure the teachers counted my name. That way the teachers wouldn't peg me as the guy who pulled the alarm. Which was a good thing, considering the fire department was probably already on its way.

No one was around to catch me as I crept to the door with the ducks and pi symbols and walked in. The teacher would have locked the door on their way out so the fire, if there was one, wouldn't spread all over the place, but this door was unlocked, thanks to the tape. I closed the door behind me. Any teachers scanning the hall would never suspect me.

Mark's red bag was right there, leaning against a desk. He'd had to leave it because teachers don't let you take your stuff with you during a fire. This would be a sleepwalk. I knelt down and started unzipping pockets.

I'm not going to do a play-by-play on this one. I found textbooks, worksheets, a pair of gym sneakers, tons of pencils . . . even a few dollars, which I *didn't* write on this time. I dug up a key, but it wasn't the master key. I sighed. If only it were that easy.

The work flew by. It wasn't until I'd zipped up Mark's backpack and leaned it back against the desk that I realized the flaw in my elegant plan.

They would be looking for me.

The teachers keep a close record of the kids in their classes, and if those kids go missing in an emergency situation, people tend to worry. A lot. Someone would be looking for me, whether the teachers outside, keeping an eye on the school doors for any stragglers, or security guards inside, crawling the halls and calling for me. If I held still, I could hear voices in the hall coming my way.

I couldn't let them catch me here. I crossed the classroom in seconds and yanked on the door handle. The door opened, but I caught myself before the door was more than cracked. Opening the door would signal my presence to anyone who might walk down this hall, and it would be hard to explain what I was doing in an eighth-grade math classroom. My lies wouldn't hold up, and Mark would win. That wasn't an option.

I was a rat in a trap, thanks to one little oversight. With as much knowledge as I had of school procedures, I should have remembered earlier that the teachers would be looking for me.

As I looked around the room, plotting my escape options, I realized that I was working on a time limit. If I didn't get out before the teachers really panicked, I'd be in trouble even if I didn't get caught here. They'd wonder why I didn't tell them I was all right and put them at ease, and that would make them mad. I also had to get out of this classroom, escaping the people in the hall, before they found me here. Best case, I'd get in trouble for hiding out in the school during a fire emergency. Worst, they'd know I pulled the fire alarm and I'd be suspended or expelled, and Mark would still win. If that happened, Becca wouldn't do a thing to back me up. She was always helpful during our after-school meetings—cameras aside—but I couldn't forget that she was, when the late-bus bell rang, my nemesis.

"The window," I whispered. It was the only way out. I just hoped I'd be able to open one without anyone seeing.

Carefully, I peeked out and looked in the hall. No one, but I could hear footsteps. I needed to act fast. I peeled the tape off the door and let it shut, locking me in. No one outside would be able to get in, which gave me a little time. Then I sprinted back across the room, leaping over the occasional chair. After climbing on a cabinet, I examined the window. Aha. Locked, but with a simple latch, and the window was big enough for someone my size to climb through. Nothing stopped me from getting out, not even a screen behind the glass. The best part was that this school is only one story high, and the drop would only be a couple feet. Also, the window faced away from the parking lot where everyone waited for the "drill" to end, so no one would see me leave the school.

I popped the latch up and pushed the window as high as I could get it to go. The window would be unlatched when teacher and class came back in, but no one would notice. In one simple maneuver I slid out the window and into the sweet freedom of the June outdoors. As I fell, I kept my hold on the lower edge of the window, reversing my fingers to the outside so I wouldn't get them caught. My weight, falling to the ground, shut the window. I was out.

I realized I was gasping for air. That had been close. Scary, but if I was being honest, I loved the surge of adrenaline that was coursing through me now. Post-job rush: better than a looping steel roller coaster mixed with an epic game of capture the flag. But I wasn't done yet—I had to find the other sixth graders and get my name counted. It's a good thing our school has a designated meeting place for the different grades.

I snuck over to the parking lot beside the running track and joined the seething mass of kids, all spreading rumors about whether there was a fire and how it started.

"There's no fire," a guy scoffed. "This is just another stupid drill."

"If it's a drill, then why are the firefighters here?" another guy asked, pointing.

I looked. Yep, there was the big red fire truck, pulling into the school parking lot. Perfect timing. Would Becca notice the firefighters and wonder what they were doing at a drill? Yes, she would. And she'd be suspicious, very suspicious. I'd have to perfect my story before I talked to her next. *I'm just as surprised as you; I searched the bag and then the alarm rang. . . .*

I pushed through the crowd until I found the cafeteria monitor, the teacher in charge of the sign-out sheet and counting students in case of an emergency. He wasn't hard to find; he was looking at a clipboard with a worried look on his face. "Excuse me," I said. "I think you missed me. My name is Jeremy Wilderson."

The teacher scanned his list, and his face softened with relief. "Yes. Did you hear me call your name?"

All innocence, I said. "No, I guess not. It's so loud out here, and I was kind of far away."

He frowned at me. "Make sure you listen better next time."

I nodded and the teacher checked off my name. Then he pulled out a walkie-talkie and walked away, saying, "We found him. He was out here the whole time."

I'd gotten out before the teachers had time to really worry. That was a plus, at least. The job was finished, but the rush was gone and I felt sick. Pulling the fire alarm had been cool, but the consequences for doing it went beyond my usual danger level, and I worried someone would realize what I'd done. I searched the crowd for Case and Hack and found them sitting on a curb.

They were talking, stealing glances my way every other second.

Great. They were already upset that I wasn't telling them about my involvement in this crime wave, and on top of that they saw me leave for something mysterious right before the fire alarm got pulled. They knew it was me; they were too smart not to. They'd have so many questions I couldn't answer, and they'd trust me even less. I wouldn't be surprised if they wondered if I really *was* the locker thief. I had to fix that . . . if I still could.

Not to mention what Becca must be thinking about me after that lucky fire drill we just had. I had to talk to her and smooth things over before she figured out what I'd done, took my actions as "going rogue," and turned me in. I wandered through the crowd, looking for her, while the firemen searched the school and declared it fire-free. As the teacher gathered us together to lead us back inside, I had to admit the obvious.

Becca wasn't there.

AS THE TEACHERS HERDED

us back into the cafeteria, Tate brushed up next to me and left a slip of paper in my hand. Without looking, I shoved it in my pocket. Cricket did the same not long later.

I had a hard time keeping my breathing steady and my hands from sweating all over the slips of paper in my pocket. I was nervous, especially when I got to the cafeteria and saw that Becca didn't show up with the rest of our class. Where was she? How could she leave me hanging in the middle of a job?

Had she known I was going to pull the alarm? Was she at that moment turning me in? I didn't know. As much as I hated to admit it, Becca was very, very smart. She must have noticed something amiss.

The whole plan had almost gone sour for me because I'd forgotten one piece of information about how teachers worked, but Becca wasn't one to forget that kind of thing. Was that her plan? Let me get caught by teachers she knew would be looking for me? I knew she wanted the key returned to the school safely, but I also knew her well enough to trust that she'd work a gambit of her own in which I got the desk next to Mark's in detention, if she could.

But that only made my next job all the more urgent. If Becca and her wonderful teachers were on their way to haul me off to detention and maybe worse, I had to find Mark's stash and find Case's and Hack's things immediately. Time to store away all the anxiety and get back to work.

Lunch ended and gym was next, giving me a perfect window. On my way to the boys' locker room, I slid Tate's and Cricket's notes out. I'd asked them, in the notes I'd written after fighting with Case and Hack, to tail Mark and see if he was ever somewhere he wasn't supposed to be. A closet or locker or room.

On that subject Tate said, *He went into the band room between classes second and third period. He's not a musician. You owe me.*

Okay, and Cricket: *I saw him loitering around the music rooms around second period. He told me to get lost when he saw me. Aren't music classes generally second and third period?*

"Thanks, guys," I whispered. One tail's word isn't

perfect, but when you have two or more, you have a place to start, and time was of the essence. I tore up both notes and threw the pieces away. Now to get out of gym class. Easy: Mark was my free pass.

Working myself up by breathing hard, I went to Coach Cread. "Coach," I said, "the locker thief stole my gym uniform. I know it was right there, in my locker, but now it's gone. I'm sorry, I'm so sorry, I should have locked it up better—"

Coach Cread doesn't handle hysteria well. He raised a hand. "Calm down, Jeremy. Show me."

I took Coach Cread to my locker, which was empty. I'd hidden my uniform under the bag in the trash can.

Coach, upon seeing the empty locker, sighed. "You can wear your regular clothes today."

"Oh, thanks." I bit my lip. "Is it okay if I go tell my mom? She'd want to know."

"She's probably teaching right now."

"She won't mind. She told me to let her know if anything of mine got stolen." I paused, acting deep in thought. "You know, I should call my dad, too. Please?"

Coach rolled his eyes. Good thing I'm an athlete; he wouldn't think I was trying to ditch class because I hated gym. "Go ahead. But be quick. We're playing knockout today."

"Great game! I'll be back as soon as I can."

I raced out of the locker room and took out my fake hall pass, just in case I got stopped. Now, on to the band room.

My skin prickled as I walked through the hallways back to the bathroom where my bag was hidden. What if Becca saw me? I was out of class without real cause after phase two was over. She'd wonder. One glance and she'd take me down. Case and Hack might never get their things back.

Why did I care, after they'd been such jerks? Let them lose their stuff! They'd see why having a retrieval specialist for a friend was so great, no matter what I decided to tell them. But I kept walking. I might consider it, but actually *not* helping Case and Hack was physically impossible.

Using a toilet to help me reach the stall's wall, I hoisted myself up and retrieved my bag. I left the books in the ceiling. The bag I took with me.

The halls of Scottsville Middle echoed with my footsteps. As nice as an empty hallway is, it makes me as obvious as a cockroach in vanilla ice cream to anyone looking. I moved quickly and quietly, my heartbeat like a timpani drum in my ears. I wondered if Mark was hiding his stash in the band room's timpani. It's big enough.

During fifth period, the band room was empty of students, though not of loose sheets of music that littered the room, interspersed with puddles of spit near the back rows of chairs. Gone was the bustle from when I'd returned Carrie's Hello Kitty wallet. I felt exposed in the open room; Becca just had to walk past, and I'd take the rap for the key theft.

"Where to start?" I muttered. The band room didn't have many crannies, but it did have a lot of cabinets. This could take all day, and I wasn't 100 percent sure Mark had stashed anything here. Tate and Cricket could have been wrong.

But standing around wouldn't get me anywhere. Looking up, I was relieved to see that the ceiling was too far up to use as a storage shed. Besides, that was *my* trick, and a stash like Mark's would be too heavy to keep that high. I wanted low and dark.

So I went to the first wall of cabinets and opened them one by one, feeling around behind replacement reeds and stacks of sheet music for anything that didn't belong. Nothing.

I moved to the second wall, at the back of the room. Locked. All of them. I stepped back and thought. I could cross these off the list; if they were locked, Mark couldn't get into them. But then again, I wasn't sure how many things the master key could unlock. I should try them anyway. I pulled my lockpick set out and searched for the right size pick.

The band room's door opened. I dropped quickly to the floor, but there was nothing else I could do. I felt open, obvious. It was a matter of time before I was caught.

"Here we are," Mark said. "Why did you want to meet here, anyway?"

Oh, my luck couldn't get any worse.

"It's quiet." Becca.

I stand—I mean *lie on the floor*—corrected.

I held my breath. I was at the back of the room, but I could see them both by the door, through the music stands and chair legs. If Becca looked across and down she'd see me. And *she* would. Most people, like the family from Case's essay job, see what they expect to see. Not Becca. She sees what is really there. She'd notice me. I had to move, but how could I move without Becca seeing?

A thick black tarp lay beside the xylophone. If only I had been over there when the door opened!

"It may be a little too quiet." Mark's feet stopped, then took a step back.

"No such thing. When a room's this quiet, I can hear everything. Even people listening in."

Like me. I held my breath.

"We have to be sure. Jeremy's contacts are every-where. I saw two of them watching me today. Why don't we go to the office, or the library, where the teachers are?"

Becca sat down in one of the black plastic chairs; its legs screeched against the floor. "If I wanted an audience for this part, I would have mentioned it to you when we were talking outside during the fire drill."

So *that's* where she had been! That no-good, lying, traitorous gumshoe.

"So, spill. I don't want to get caught here," Mark said.

"I thought you had permission to miss English to talk to me."

"I do," Mark said quickly. "But the band room's kind of a nerdy place, don't you think?"

"Never thought about it."

I let my breath out in a thin, slow stream. I thought Becca heard, she was so quiet, but then she said, "Wilder-son's been targeting you, specifically." Her voice, when she said my name, sounded unusually acidic.

"Yeah. I think he went through my backpack."

"Seems like he feels threatened by you. You don't, by any chance, know where he keeps his stash?"

"His stash." Mark leaned against a music stand, top-pling it.

As it crashed to the floor, I took the opportunity to roll toward the tarp. My backpack scratched against the linoleum.

"What was that?" Becca asked. I huddled under the tarp, praying for instant invisibility.

"I knocked over a stand," Mark said.

"I heard that. I heard something else, too."

"This room echoes. What, you think Jeremy is in here?"

"He wouldn't dare." Becca's voice was a poison dart. I shivered.

"Maybe we should check."

Silence. "No. It must have been an echo." I didn't like the steely edge in Becca's voice. I could see why she wouldn't trap me with Mark there; it might clue him in to our game. But after he left, she'd search and find me. She wouldn't stop until she did.

I had to move. I had to get to a closet or out a window. Even under the tarp I was too exposed. If Becca changed perspective, she could see me. The door to the band's locker room was open. That little room was full of cubbies and deep crannies. The ceiling even had a cracked tile that was easy to move and to see through. It was hiding-place heaven. But how could I get there? I lowered the edge of the tarp and watched Becca and Mark with one eye.

Becca folded her arms. "So, do you have anything to tell me?"

"About what?"

"About Jeremy's stash. He can't leave campus during school, so when he steals—"

"He has to hide it all in the school somewhere. I get it." Mark sat down backward on a chair. "Why do you think I know?"

Becca shrugged. "I'm covering my bases. Jeremy seems to be targeting you. First your locker, now your backpack . . . I think maybe you know something and he's attacking you to silence you."

"I don't know anything."

"You sure?" Becca's voice had the kind of glee I always enjoyed hearing used on someone else. I would have enjoyed it more if I hadn't been about to get caught.

An idea came to me. Moving a millimeter at a time, I reached down and slid off one shoe.

Becca stood up. I took the noise she made as cover to slip the other shoe off. "It just seems odd that he would target *you*. You're not in our grade, and as far as I know, you and Jeremy aren't on any teams or in clubs together. Why you?"

"How should I know how a thief's mind works?"

"You shouldn't. So you're telling me you don't know where the stash is?"

"No idea."

I could feel Becca smile. A smirk was not only audible but also tangible, then. Disturbing. "Thank you for your help. Let me know if you have anything else." Becca waved at the door. "Go ahead and get out of this nerdy room."

Mark didn't move. His eyes flicked to the back of the room. I froze—did he see me?—but his gaze swept back to Becca's face. "You should get back too."

"I will. But after you." Becca led Mark to the door.

"You'll be late for class."

"I've got a free pass for the whole period. Don't worry about me. I'm going to check out that sound I heard."

"Let me help."

"Who's the detective here? Go. It will only take a minute."

He protested, but it's hard to argue with a tiny monster like Becca. When he was gone, she strode to the xylophone tarp and yanked it up.

But I was gone. While she and Mark had debated about who should leave first, I'd stayed low and moved fast, carrying my shoes in my hand. My socks had muffled the sound of my footsteps. Their distraction had been enough to let me get to the band locker room door, which was open.

Becca narrowed her eyes and looked around. I crouched in the shadow of the locker room door, nestled between the door and the small instrument cubbies. The floor was cold and a little wet under my socks. Spit. Great.

The band room door opened again, and Becca dropped to the floor. Behind the tarp. Her turn to sweat and hide. So there was justice in the world after all.

Mark stepped inside. How did I know it was him when I couldn't see? He'd been uneasy in the band room because it was where his stash was. Becca had probably taken him there just to watch him squirm. She was looking for the stash too and had used his guilt as a giveaway. Mark, on edge, had come back to make sure his stash was undisturbed.

His footsteps stopped, and then he walked into the locker room. I squeezed against the wall, deeper into the shadows, as Mark walked closer and closer.

If I slipped out, Becca would catch me. But if Mark got any closer, *he'd* catch me. I held my breath, hoping for a miracle.

To my amazement, Mark stopped. He stood beside a large cubby meant for tubas or something. He reached in, pulled back, smiled, and left. I heard the band room door close as he made his exit.

So that was where the stash was. Perfect.

I peered through the crack between the door and frame. Becca stood up. Not wasting a second and using the cubbies as a ladder, I climbed up to the ceiling. I pushed aside the cracked tile to reveal the large pipe above it. I tested its strength with a sharp pull. It held. With the grace of an acrobat, I grabbed the pipe and hoisted myself up, wrapping my legs around the pipe. I hung there like a sloth, moving only to slide the tile back into place.

Through the crack I could see everything. Becca entered through the locker room door and looked around.

"Come out, Wilderson."

Like that was going to happen. I hugged the pipe tighter. I'd found this hiding space when I'd returned a lost bottle of slide oil, but this was my first time trying it out. Good thing the pipe wasn't scalding hot; some were.

Becca walked past all the cubbies large enough to hold me. Twice. And then a third time. She stopped by the one with Mark's stash. Reaching in, she moved something. I watched as she took out her camera and snapped a couple of pictures.

She closed the door on the stash and looked around the locker room again. "I know you're here. We have things to *talk about*." When I (obviously) didn't answer, she sighed, shook her head, and left the locker room, closing the door behind her.

I didn't move. Becca was tricky.

She hadn't left. The door opened and Becca walked back in. She scanned the cubbies again, and then her eyes crept up, up, up . . . to the cracked ceiling tile. She grinned in a way that made my skin burn as if the pipe had been hot. Her hand gripped a cubby like a rung.

"Becca! Becca Mills!" Becca turned.

"What is it?" She sounded angry and kept glancing up at the ceiling.

Multiple voices, talking over each other. They echoed in the room and were muffled by the ceiling. "I need your help. Now."

"The Flash has gone missing."

"Ms. Finnegan is really upset. We told her you'd be able to help.

"Come on! Please. It's your job."

Becca sighed. She cast one last look in my general direction and left. A minute passed and I breathed easier. I slid the tile back and dropped out of the ceiling. After a short descent I was back on terra firma and wondering what had just happened.

The Flash is the life sciences room's turtle. It likes to

hide under the sawdust in its terrarium. I doubted Ms. Finnegan was really upset. What had happened? Weird that the call for help had come just in time to save me.

I'd have to think about it later when I wasn't in the middle of a job. Time to work. The cubby Mark had favored held a trumpet case (strange, for such a large space) and the jacket of a band uniform. I checked for booby traps, dismantled one that involved a green paint balloon, then set the trumpet case on the floor and removed the jacket.

There it was. The stash. Case's forged hall passes tied in a bundle, Hack's mom's tablet, my books and pens, as well as a bunch of other stolen goods. Not a moment to lose. As fast as I could, I swept the entire stash into my backpack. When the locker was empty, I threw in the crumpled note with the winky face Mark had left in my locker. I grinned as I set the jacket down on top of it and replaced the trumpet case.

My backpack bounced on my back, heavy and bulky, as I hurried back to gym class. I'd like to tell you my heart was the opposite, as light and airy as Silly String, but it wasn't. The stash, as big as it was, was only a small part of Mark's take. Who knew where the rest was?

On top of that, Becca knew I had been in there. I knew she did; she was too good a detective not to know.

She also had to know that I had pulled the fire alarm to get into Mark's stuff. As I hid my backpack in the ceiling of the boys' locker room for added security, I wondered what she'd do the next time I saw her.

Probably kill me.

13

I HAD TRACK PRACTICE AFTER
school, and since we had a meet scheduled for the next day, the coach pushed us extra hard. I literally didn't have time to breathe as he made us sprinters practice our dashes over and over.

Finally Coach Cread yelled, "Okay, sprinters, that's enough. Run one more mile and stretch." Yes, I know. Another mile to end practice. He likes all his runners to have some long-distance endurance. Also he's a sadist.

As we began our last four laps around the track, I made eye contact with one of my teammates and rolled my eyes in my best Becca Mills impression. He snorted, since laughing took too much air. Then his grin became a frown. This teammate had come to me complaining of a locker theft. A stolen pair of sneakers, if I remembered right. He passed me, leaving me to remember that my clients doubted me, even wondered if I was the thief. The sooner Becca and I took down Mark, the better.

As I rounded my second lap, I saw Becca herself practicing with the shot put. Speak of the devil.

I really, really didn't want to talk to her. But I had to face her sooner or later. And, if I acted now, I could more easily convince her I was innocent. Then again, I didn't think she'd believe me. She knew I had pulled the alarm and had been sneaking around in the band room. She probably wanted to get all bad cop and no good cop, preferably in a small room with one bright light shining right in my eyes. More so than usual.

Self-preservation won out: I'd avoid her for as long as I could. I finished my run and stretched, just like Coach ordered, all the while keeping my untrustworthy partner in my sight.

Becca didn't look my way at all during practice. Then, when I got up to get water and stretch by the fence, she was somehow right behind me. "Hello, Wilderson." Her voice could cause frostbite.

I took a deep breath, prepared a sunny smile, and turned around. "Hey, partner. Phase two down, one phase to go. I think it's going well."

"What makes you think that?" Becca was deadly calm.

"This part of the job's over, I'm still here, and you're

still here. No one's in detention or flattened in the parking lot. In my line of work that means a job well done."

"Yeah, about that. Don't you think we got a little *too* lucky today?"

"Define 'too lucky.' Not something I normally encounter." I policed my every movement, pretending nothing was wrong. The accusation was coming. I could feel Becca winding up, getting ready to take the shot and knock me out.

"During the fire drill, I saw Mark coming out without his backpack. I also saw a bunch of fire trucks. They don't come for drills, because the school warns them ahead of time that it's all fake, so that was weird. You know what I didn't see? You."

"What are you saying?" I was sick of her playing games. Just accuse me already and get it over with!

Becca stepped closer to me. "This is what's going to happen. You're going to, very honestly, assure me that you had nothing to do with today's pulled alarm. That you were surprised but that you used it to your advantage. That you did not *break the law* after promising me you wouldn't."

"Maybe no one pulled the alarm. Maybe there was a real fire in the cafeteria."

Becca pushed me. "Stop it. Do you think I'm an idiot? Tell me the truth, Wilderson."

"There're lots of truths in the world. Which one do you want?"

"Stop it now!" Becca was shaking. "I trusted you, you know that? And then you go and pull the alarm. Don't tell me you didn't. The alarm was pulled; the teachers know. They saw that it had been pulled down. And right after I left you? Didn't you think I'd put it together?"

The game was over. "We needed an opening. We weren't going to get one unless I made it myself. So I did."

"What was all that about getting to Mark's backpack during his class?"

"A lie. Me, search a bag in front of Mark and the rest of his class? Without getting anybody suspicious? Are you kidding?"

"So you lie to me, and then you pull the fire alarm. You can't stop, can you? You can't be honest for one day. You're addicted to lawbreaking and deceit. And don't even get me started on the whole band-room thing."

"What band-room thing?"

"Don't. Just don't. Remind me, Wilderson, what were the terms of my agreeing to work with you on this?"

"While we work together, I don't retrieve at all, and I tell you everything. If I break our agreement, you'll turn me in. Am I missing anything?"

"So you'll understand, then, when I turn you in Monday morning for everything you did?"

I thought of Case and Hack and their distrust in me, which got my blood running as hot as the blacktop on a summer's day. I turned that anger like a fire hose on the detective. "Turn me in? I have done nothing but help you stop Mark. I thought that was the important thing right now."

Becca slammed me against the chain-link fence, her lip curled. "There's a right and wrong way to do things. I'm having a hard time even looking at you because of the fire alarm. I can believe you think you did it for the right reasons, but then you go and betray my trust even more by stealing. I know you were in the band room today. Why else would your two crooked friends send me on a wild turtle chase when I was seconds away from catching you?"

Case and Hack did what now? So it was them I'd heard earlier.

"I'm not speaking to them," I said, tamping down my confusion and other, more complicated emotions. Why would they help me when they'd made it clear they thought I didn't trust them enough to rely on them? Case had flat-out said he wouldn't help me if I ran into trouble.

"Well, maybe they'll be on better terms with you after you do time for faking a fire." Becca pulled on my shirt, ready to make a citizen's arrest.

I peeled Becca's hands off my collar. "Not doing the time."

"Yes, you are. You broke our agreement, so you're going to pay the price. You pulled the alarm, and I know you were stealing today."

I looked her in the eyes. "Prove it."

Her face turned red. She couldn't, and she knew it. "I just know," she said, her voice strained.

"Why? Because you hate me? That's a good reason. Do you think Principal McDuff is going to accept that as enough evidence to suspend me?"

Becca spat on the ground. "Nothing ever sticks to you, Wilderson. Ever."

"Maybe it's karma for trying to do the right thing."

"And what is the right thing? According to you?"

"Stopping Mark. Which means us working in sync. I need you for this, and you need me for phase three. We have to keep moving forward together."

Becca looked flustered. I'd gotten to her. I'd reminded her that she didn't have anything that would stand as evidence incriminating me except her word against mine. Then I'd played the "you need me" card. Mark couldn't go free, and she needed my help to stop him. We both knew that.

We stood, silent, awkwardly trying to figure out

where to go next. Then Becca spoke. "Why do you do this, Jeremy?"

It was the first time she'd ever called me by my first name. "Do what?"

"This. Lie, steal, break the rules." Becca's voice was quiet, and her icy gaze had melted to the ground.

It should have felt great, beating Becca like this, but it didn't. I should have felt elated. Instead I felt dirty.

I exhaled loudly, like I'd run an extra mile. "Because sometimes the rules hurt more than they help."

Becca shook her head. "That's not true. What you're doing . . . it hurts people a lot more than you think it does. The teachers are looking for the person who pulled the fire alarm. If they don't catch you, they'll catch someone else. Someone innocent."

I hadn't thought of that. My skin crawled, picturing an innocent person getting blamed for the crime I'd committed.

"You don't know that."

She sighed. "Actually, I do. They always find someone. But I guess, in the meantime, we have phase two over and done."

"Backpack is clean, but I did run into a little trouble. I forgot they'd send the security guards looking for me."

"Climbed out a window, though, right?" I nodded,

and she gave me a weary smile. "See? There's the master thief I know and distrust."

"Was that almost a compliment?"

"Almost." Becca kicked at the grass. She looked at me with a solemn expression. "I should turn you in for the fire alarm, just so no one else gets blamed. I really should. You'd be in so much trouble."

"Yeah? How much?"

"Oh, suspended for sure. Maybe expelled, if they could link the missing key and all those thefts to you." Becca smiled, her face looking as dreamy and distant as Rick's when he imagines winning the state championship. It didn't boost my confidence.

I turned the conversation back to where I wanted it. "Yeah, and the key would stay missing and Mark would get away with it. Maybe we should wait until the key is on the janitor's ring before getting back to our game of cops and robbers."

"I'm the cop, right?"

"Of course you're the cop. Seriously. What else could you be?"

"Good point. And after this is over, I am going to bring you down. I'll find evidence. I'm learning a lot about your method and, as impressive as it is, it can't work forever."

"Was that another compliment? Stop before I drop dead."

She laughed. "I can admire skill, even if I don't like how that skill is used. Now get lost, thief, before someone notices we're talking and it gets back to Mark."

"Don't want him to know the cop and robber are working together?"

She grinned. "My reputation would be shattered."

"Well, you better start sweeping up the pieces, because we've been chatting for a while over here. Everyone must have seen by now. Wonder what they're thinking?" I leaned in close and whispered, "Maybe they think we're secretly dating."

Oh yeah, I was back! Safe, for the moment, and bantering with the girl who was out to get me, just like nothing had happened.

Still smiling, Becca placed one hand on my shoulder. "Oh, I'm not sweeping up anything, Wilderson," she said sweetly. "Not when there's still time for damage control."

"Oh yeah? What kind of damage control?" I leaned in closer, raising my eyebrows.

Without warning she yanked hard on my shoulder, spinning me around. Something hard and blunt—like a foot—hit me in my back, and I went sprawling forward onto the grass.

"That kind," Becca said amid scattered laughter. "And you were right, they were watching." She leaned down. "That's for the fire alarm and everything you're not telling me. I do need you if I'm ever going to bring Mark down. But as soon as we've got him, I'm going to turn you in for the fire alarm and anything else I can find. A weekend is long enough to gather the evidence I need." She straightened up and walked away.

So, *not* back to normal.

I should have been mad. I should have been worried. I should have started to plan how I would protect myself from Becca's accusations, which I knew would fly right up to Principal McDuff as soon as the key was hanging on its hook in the janitor's closet once more. But though I'd never admit it, I sat up with a little smile tugging at my lips.

Hey, I can admire skill, even if I don't like how that skill is being used, right?

14

AFTER TRACK PRACTICE I
retrieved my backpack, full of Mark's stash, from its hiding place in the school. I had kept it inside so Becca couldn't rifle through it during a water break and find the proof she needed to turn me in.

My stomach felt crumpled as I carried the backpack home, matched the stolen goods to the list, and packed everything on my bike to return it. The thought of the grateful looks on the poor victims' faces didn't raise my spirits. What was this?

Was Becca right when she said that I hurt people with what I did? That couldn't be true. I helped. I didn't steal anything; I retrieved it. I didn't break anything when I worked. Lots of people needed what I could give them.

The fire alarm, though. If someone else was blamed for the alarm being pulled? That would be my fault.

Fire alarms were a big deal. Teachers worked hard to catch any kid who pulled one without good reason. Their punishment would be harsh enough to damage an innocent person for life, or at least until graduation.

I tried to ignore the weird, guilty squirm in my gut as I returned all the stolen items on my list. When I got to the last two, I took a deep breath. This had to be done.

I knocked on Hack's door. His mom worked late on Fridays and thus couldn't enforce his grounding, so I knew Case would be over, escaping his sisters and playing video games. Probably Madden, until Hack got bored of it and they moved on to racing games. It's where I would have been if I was still on good terms with them and not working.

Hack answered the door. When he saw me, he raised an eyebrow. "Hey, J."

"Hey." I took off my almost-empty backpack and pulled out the tablet.

Hack's hand moved faster than the snap of a rubber band, taking the tablet from me. "You got it back."

"It's my job."

"J? What are you doing here?" Case appeared behind Hack as I pulled the bundle of hall passes from my bag.

"A peace offering," I said. "And a thank-you."

"You don't have to thank us for anything." Case set the passes down inside the door.

"Yes, I do. I heard what you did for me. How is the Flash, by the way?"

"Safe and sound." Case grinned. "Our local detective is very good. Did you know that Ms. Finnegan's turtle likes to bury itself in its sawdust?"

"*I* most certainly didn't," Hack said, eyes wide with mock innocence. "We're so lucky to have the snitch's superior deductive skills."

I laughed. "Again, thanks."

"You're still our friend," Hack said. "Even if you don't let us in on everything." He looked at the tablet. "Though when we saw you disappear before the fire drill, I have to admit, it looked like you'd gone dirty. Not that we believe that, of course," he finished.

"I haven't gone bad," I said. "I promise."

"Oh, we know," Hack said. "Didn't you hear? Tomboy Tate pulled the fire alarm."

I felt like my bones were being sucked out of my body. "What?"

"Tate did it. One of the eighth-grade math teachers saw her loitering in the hall suspiciously. Principal McDuff had her brought down to the office. They called her parents."

Uh-oh. Becca had been right. The teachers had found a suspect and blamed her for what I'd done. The worst part was that Tate was probably skulking in the halls because I'd asked her to, trying to get information about Mark's stash. It was my fault, twice over, that she was in trouble: Not only was Tate in trouble for something I did, but it was also me who made sure she looked guilty enough to blame. I had to make it right.

But how on earth could I fix this? What could I give the principal to make him let Tate go?

"What's up, J?" Case asked. "You look sick. Do you and Tate have, you know, a thing? Because if you do, I'll back off."

"What? No. There's no thing."

"It's about the job, isn't it?" Hack asked. "What's happening?"

I swallowed. "I'm glad you know I haven't gone dirty. I want to tell you everything. But I can't tell you any more than I already have."

"Why not?" Case, this time. His arms were folded, but his face was listening.

"It's a long story." I looked at my feet. "I'm not keeping you in the dark because I don't trust you. There's no one I'd rather talk to than you. But after today, you must have seen the kind of trouble I'm in; you even helped me get out of some of it. It's worse than you know, and I know you'd help me if I asked or even if I didn't. So I won't tell you anything. You can't help with something you don't know about." Hack opened his mouth to argue, and I headed him off. "No. Not with this. I'm not going to budge."

I thought of Becca and the way she was going to turn me in for the retrieving and the fire alarm, and I thought about Tate, sitting in the principal's office, punished for a crime she didn't commit. "There's a good chance I'm going to go down for this one," I said. "You're not going down with me."

"We can help," Hack said. "Whatever you need."

"We're here for you," Case said.

It felt good to hear them say that. "I know. Don't fight me on this. I have to finish this alone."

"You won't go down," Hack said. "You're too good. No one has anything on you."

I nodded, thinking about Becca again and deciding to never tell my friends about my deal with her. "You're probably right. Anyway, thanks again for saving me. How did you know I was in the band room?"

Case shrugged. "Cricket told us what he told you. We thought it would be a good chance to confront you—"

"See for ourselves what you weren't telling us," Hack added.

"Then we saw Becca and some eighth grader inside.

He left; she didn't. We heard her calling for you. So we gave her a reason to leave."

"Thanks." I didn't feel like I could say that enough times to make it mean something.

"No, thank you." Hack raised the tablet. "Wanna come in and own Case at Mario Kart a few times before my mom comes home? Someone has to, and I'm getting bored."

Case rolled his eyes. "Last player gets the blue shells. It's all about strategy."

"So why haven't you won a single game?"

I waved. "Still here. Sounds like fun, but I'm working. See you next week?" *If I'm still free.*

Case nodded, an odd look in his dark eyes. "Sure, next week."

Hack grinned. "Later, J."

I nodded and went home, having returned all the stolen items. My stomach twisted as I thought about Tate and what I had to do. There had to be a way to help her without turning myself in. But I couldn't think of what it was.

At least I had other things to think about. Mark wouldn't be able to get inside the school for the weekend, so I had time to plan and execute the third and last phase of getting back the master key. Becca had agreed to keep working with me because this last phase required all of my skills. Everything I knew how to do would come into play in a way a private eye couldn't imitate. But for the time being I had to balance waiting with action.

Easier said than done. Within an hour of coming home and having my customary fight with Rick, I itched to go over to Becca's and run some ideas by her. But that was a bad idea for many reasons. One: Even after she kicked me in the back, someone might suspect we had some kind of partnership, and I couldn't let anyone think that. It might get back to Case and Hack, and although everything seemed to be okay between us again, all that hard work would shatter if they knew I was working with the gumshoe. Talk about not trusting me *then*.

Two: Yes, we had a deal, and although she was mad at me about pulling the fire alarm, she'd seemed okay after we talked at practice. Still, I didn't know how I would manage a conversation with her. She's a detective. They have to be good actors to get what they need from people. Watch TV sometime and you'll see what I mean. Just by talking to her, I could give her the evidence she needed to turn me in and make it stick. All it would take would be her camera hidden better than last time.

Although, would that be such a bad thing? Once Mark was taken care of, maybe I had some debts to pay. *What you're doing . . . it hurts people.*

I banished the ghostly echo of Becca's voice. I couldn't afford to think like that. Focus on Mark: That was the key. But the achy feeling lingered. Tate was in trouble and it was my fault. I owed her for the help she'd given me, tailing Mark. Even without that debt I couldn't let her take the fall for me.

But what could I do? Mark was on the loose and I had to stop him.

After an hour of sitting in my room, guilt-crazy and playing a game of catch with my wall, I was more than glad to hear a knock at the back door. "I've got it!" I yelled down the stairs.

I tossed the tennis ball into a pile of dirty clothes and ran downstairs in record time. Rick had answered the back door for me.

"Looks like you're in trouble now, Dr. Evil," he said, smiling as he walked away. "Don't stay out too late."

Was it Becca? Teachers? But why would teachers come after me on Friday night and come to the *back* door?

I pulled the door open farther and saw, to my extreme disappointment, Mark. He was flanked by two huge guys who were clearly going to go on to play high school football before getting jobs as prison guards. That is, if they didn't end up as inmates for shattering someone's kneecaps.

"Good to see you again," Mark said. "I was just talking to your brother. Seems like a nice guy."

"He's a meathead," I said. "But I guess you have a thing for those."

"What, these guys?" Mark laughed. "Sean and Hugo are harmless. They just wanted to come along and meet the great Jeremy Wilderson themselves."

"I doubt that. It's nice, though, that business is so good that you can afford a pair. Me, I've never had any need to buy bravery. So," I said, clapping my hands together. "What can I do for you fine gentlemen? Steal an old lady's life savings? Kidnap a toddler's pet kitty?"

Mark smirked. "I didn't take you for the bitter kind, Jeremy. I just thought you and I could go for a little walk."

I would have rather stapled my fingers together, but I had no choice but to go with him. Mark's newly bought thugs would make sure I cooperated. But there was a silver lining to this meeting: If Mark was getting up close and personal . . .

"I must really have you scared," I said. I turned my head and called back into the house, "Mom, I'm going outside."

"Okay. Dinner's in an hour!"

I looked at Mark. "Dinner's in an hour. If I'm not back by then, she'll worry."

"Don't do anything stupid and you will be back by then. We're running out of time."

I stretched out my arms. "Where to?"

"Around."

We left my backyard in silence. I tried to lead the group to the sidewalk so Becca could maybe, possibly see me, but the unfortunately named Hugo put an arm around me and steered me into the woods behind my house. *Hugo.* No wonder he'd turned to crime.

Once we were so far into the trees that I couldn't hear the neighborhood traffic anymore, Sean shoved me from behind, throwing me facedown into dirt and shredded tree bark. *Second time today,* I thought as I pushed myself to a kneeling position. Or tried to, I should say. Hugo, pushed down on my back with his foot. Not meant to hurt, but where I lay, pressed against the ground, a few fallen twigs scratched my face. Becca's kick had been downright chiropractic compared to this.

Mark knelt next to me. "How does it feel to be under my boot?"

"Technically, it's not your boot; it's Hugo's."

"He works for me, so it's the same thing. Listen to me, kid. Nice trick taking my stash today, but as of right now you're going to stop this little witch hunt of yours."

"It's not a witch hunt. If it were, I'd be hunting you

and not the key. A lot of innocent people would also be in trouble. I'd call this more Robin Hood–style vigilante-justice."

"Will you stop analyzing my threats?" Mark snapped his fingers, and one of the thugs—Sean, I think—kicked my side. Not painful, but annoying. Hugo took his foot off me and, when I started to get up, grabbed my hair and jerked my head back. That time it hurt. One thick arm snaked across my throat in a choke hold. I didn't think anybody under eighteen (whose mother wasn't a cop) was allowed to learn that.

"Careful, boys," Mark said. "He can't do what we want if he winds up in the hospital."

Hugo released me. Rubbing my neck for dramatic effect, I coughed and wheezed. Then I stopped. "It wasn't that bad," I said in my normal voice. "Next time, stop the arteries. I'll pass out in no time."

Looking at Mark, I added, "I have to admit, this is the most exciting job I've ever done. Even better than the one where Caleb Vanderhoos lost his retainer on the Natural History Museum field trip and I only had a half hour to track it down. And while I'm grateful for you keeping your rabid dogs from tearing me apart, I have to wonder why. If I'm out of the picture, the pressure on you goes away."

"Maybe not from you, no, but what about your partner?" Mark smirked. "I know you have one; there's no way you could get into my locker and backpack without getting caught unless someone was helping you."

I smirked back, which made a new scratch on my cheek sting. I'd have to clean that as soon as I got home. "I don't have a partner." *I have a warden.*

Mark's face turned bright red. "You do! I know you do."

I laughed. He looked just like Becca when she was accusing me of retrieving in the band room and pulling the fire alarm. The thought made my stomach twinge but my heart leap. If I'd bested the school's number-one private eye, a petty thief was no trouble.

"No partner."

"I know there's one. Who is it? Sean, Hugo, persuade him for me."

"'Persuade him for me'? Really? Where'd you learn that, a made-for-TV spy thriller?" I raised my hands. "It's not going to do you any good."

And it wouldn't; I'd won before we'd begun. So what if I was outnumbered and in danger of a little roughing up? Mark may have realized I had a partner, but he would sooner believe in little goblins that eat toenails with maple syrup than that I'd team up with Becca Mills. I could tell the truth and he wouldn't buy it. It was one perk of working with her; she was so far removed from me that she was invisible on Mark's radar.

"I don't have a partner," I said with as much scorn as I could muster. "You hired me because I'm the best, and the best work alone. It's not my fault if that's hard for an amateur like you to believe."

Hugo clenched his fist. "Hold on," Mark said. "We're not done yet."

He leaned in close to where I knelt on the ground. "You aren't the best. I am."

I flopped down and reclined on my stomach, face in my hands, looking up at him like I was watching a mildly interesting caterpillar eating a buttercup. "You're small-time, Mark. Strictly small-time."

Mark's face muscles twitched. "Small-time? I've stolen more in the past two days than you have in your whole career."

"Then why are you so scared?" I grinned. "These meteoric—nice word, right?—rises to the top are fragile. Sure, people are noticing you now, but all this could go away fast if the key, the source of your power, disappears. You can't let that happen."

His lips twisting, Mark grabbed my head and drove my face into the ground. "You found nothing when you looked in my locker and my backpack," he said. "*Nothing*.

It's not there. I beat you, Wilderson. I won. Do you call that small-time? Now you need to call your partner and tell him it's over. If you don't, the principal is going to get a *very* interesting surprise on Monday."

Uh-oh. I knew what that meant: framing time. It was one thing for Becca to bring me in for things I actually *did*, but it was another entirely for Mark to accuse me of being behind the crime wave he'd committed. I pushed my face out of the dirt and resumed kneeling. "I'm going to find the key. You can't stop me."

Mark stepped back. "Maybe not you. But I can stop your partner. I'll find out who it is, and he'll be sorry he ever agreed to work with you."

"What, are you going to watch me? Guess I'm wearing my swim trunks in the shower tonight."

Sean's fist landed on my shoulder. It hurt, but it wasn't meant to damage anything. Not an attack, but a warning.

Mark waved, and both thugs hauled me up by my arms. "Let's get you home for dinner. Don't want your mommy getting worried."

They marched me home, where I rushed to the bathroom to clean my scratches. Nothing too bad, but that punch on the shoulder was going to bruise. I'd have to make sure Mom didn't see it. The scratches, on the other hand, cleaned up well, but Mom's trained eye would zero in on them as if they were flashing green and red.

I mean, even Rick noticed them. "Look at this. The criminal mastermind got himself roughed up," he said. His voice sounded oddly serious.

"I tripped and fell. It happens."

Rick gave me a long look. "For future reference, if you want anyone to believe you, you'll need to come up with a better story. Maybe one that factors in the way you're favoring that shoulder. Let me have full control of the TV tonight and I'll tell Mom I was teaching you football."

"She won't believe it."

He shrugged. "Try me. And is it a deal or not?"

I sighed. "It's a deal."

"Great." He turned and walked back to his room.

I went to mine, preparing to spend the entire evening there while Rick watched whatever inane action show or brain-dead sports he wanted. Becca, Mark, Rick—I couldn't win!

15

MOM, OF COURSE, ASKED

about the scratches on my face, and Rick stepped in with a lie about tossing a football around in the yard and my eating it in the shrubs. Like it or not, I had to agree with whatever he said. Good thing people trust lies that sound embarrassing. Mom asked a few questions, but in the end she bought the whole thing.

After dinner I sat on my bed. I ached all over and, believe it or not, also worried that I was playing with fire. Okay, so I *was* playing with fire, but it felt like the flames were leaping all around me and my fire extinguisher had turned out to be a flamethrower and I couldn't ask for help because some *moron* had already gone and pulled the fire alarm.

The idea *was* to make sure Mark knew I was coming after him, but I hadn't expected to get beaten up in the woods. And Mark had made it clear that sending thugs my way wasn't even the worst he could do. What would he tell the principal if I didn't let up the chase? What would happen to me? What would he do to *Becca* if he found out I was working with her?

I shouldn't care. Let Becca take care of Mark or vice versa. It would solve my problems.

But Jeremy Wilderson didn't work that way. I had to solve my own problems. Besides, letting Mark and Becca attack each other while I stood by eating Milk Duds was . . . wrong.

I stood up and paced my room. I wanted to talk to someone, but who? It wasn't like I could bare my soul to Rick, who'd laugh, or Mom, who'd try to understand but wouldn't, not without my explaining that I'd been retrieving all year.

I walked to the hall and picked up our cordless phone. My fingers tapped out the first six digits of Case's number. He would have had to leave Hack's house before Hack's mom came home, so he would be at home after having a good time playing video games and possibly doing whipped cream mouth shots. But I stopped because I remembered that "having a good time" meant not having scratches or bruises thanks to poor work choices.

Case and Hack were my friends and the obvious

choice for my partners. If I was being watched—and I knew Mark would keep a close eye on my activities—then calling Case and Hack would put my friends on the bad guy's radar. In fact the goons were probably there already; I'd have to stay far away from my friends until the job was done if I wanted to keep them safe. If I was worried about Becca—and weirdly, I was—the anxiety for her was tiny compared to my worry that Mark would harm my best friends. When all this was over, I'd be free and clear to explain everything to them (minus my involvement with Becca), as long as I did it after my stint in in-school suspension/grounding.

But someone needed to know I'd been threatened. I canceled the call, went downstairs, found the number I wanted in the neighborhood parents' contact list, and then returned to my room. I had to call Becca, but I had to be extra sneaky about it.

Okay, here's the thing. Being extra sneaky does not mean hiding items behind your back or carrying phones into locked rooms. It can, if you do those things often, but most people don't. Being extra sneaky is acting like everything is normal when it's not. For example, it would be weird for me to sneak up to my room with a phone under my shirt and call someone. It would be normal, however, for me to call a friend from school about an assignment.

Sneaky behavior was a go. I put the phone back in its cradle and went into my room, where my backpack waited. Homework time. I had to anyway; it was house rules the Friday before a Saturday track meet. It also made a good show for anyone watching the house.

I pulled out my math binder and started filling in the answers for that night's worksheet. After about fifteen minutes, I flipped through my binder like I was looking for something, and then I walked out to the phone. I know, I know: The odds that someone was watching me right then, as I did homework in my room, were astronomical. But as long as there was a chance, I had to be careful.

I went back out to the phone.

My fingers tightened and shook the phone as I raised it to my ear. Becca needed to know, right now, what Mark had said to me . . . wait. No. What if she was working with him to get me? I mean, that was her cover for the job—making Mark think she was after me—but what if it wasn't a cover? What if it was real and *I* was the unwitting mark in her elaborate con? If I told her how freaked out Mark's visit had made me, she might tell him, and the plan would be ruined. Well, it would be ruined anyway if Becca told him everything, but still. I wouldn't be able to run any kind of backup plan.

I took a deep breath. Okay, I was losing control. I needed to be rational. Becca would never work with Mark; as much as she hated me, he was the bigger threat. I knew she had her own agenda separate from mine or Mark's. She'd told me as much. When the job was done, I'd be next up for the guillotine. I'd have to figure out the right thing to do about that when all this was over. But, at the moment, I dialed Becca's number.

Her mom answered the phone.

I swallowed. "Hello, Detective Mills, is Becca there?"

"She is. May I ask who's calling?"

"Jeremy." I thought about adding my last name, but I bet Becca had mentioned me as Wilderson, once or twice, to her cop mother. In this case, I didn't want my reputation to precede me.

"I'll go get her."

A moment later Becca's voice said, "Hey, thief boy."

Of course she'd say that. "Hey, snitch. So, you'll never believe who I talked to today."

"Your parole officer?"

"Ha-ha. I'm doing that right now. No, Mark came over and warned me what was in store if me *and my partner* didn't give up looking for the key."

Becca said something, but the static over the phone was too much and I must have misheard.

"What was that?"

"I said, 'Are you okay?' One of my sources saw him walking with a couple of eighth-grade thugs. If he was going to talk to you, I'd guess you got a little roughed up."

I touched a scratch on my face. "Not too bad. The whole thing was supposed to scare me. But since when do you care about how I'm feeling?"

"I don't. It's just . . . if I lose you now, phase three never happens and the plan falls apart. Don't break your leg on me."

"Is it just me or did you sound legitimately concerned for my health?"

"Just you."

I wasn't convinced, but I said, "Must be a bad connection."

"Or Mark rattled your brain, if you ever had one to begin with." After some silence Becca coughed. "Uh, so, what did he say?"

"Oh, right. He knows I have a partner, but don't worry, he doesn't know it's you. He'd never suspect you. But he's watching me, Becca. He's trying to find out who's working with me. He also said he hid the key somewhere I can never find it."

"Right. Well, it sounds like your plan is working."

"That's a very optimistic way of looking at it."

"You know I'm right. We'll have the key soon. By Monday, probably. Then I get to turn you both in."

"That reminds me . . ." I decided against telling her about the surprisingly complicated emotions I'd been having regarding her turning me in. Instead I said, "There's something else Mark said. He told me that if I didn't stop looking for the key, he'd give something to the principal on Monday. Something that would incriminate me."

"Really? He said that?"

"No, not in so many words, but he implied it pretty hard."

"Like, fist-or-foot hard?"

"Just about."

"Yeesh. Did he say what it was?"

"No. Could you—"

"I'm on it," Becca said. "And it's probably a good idea if we don't visit each other until this is over."

"I get that you don't want anyone to see you with me and think you're a dirty cop, but we still need to talk about phase three," I said. I considered telling her about Tate, but the thought left such a sour taste in my mouth that I couldn't bring myself to mention it.

Besides, I knew what Becca would say. She'd want me to turn myself in, get Tate out of trouble by confessing. I could do that, but it meant giving up everything I'd built over the last year. My work. My legacy. Everything. I couldn't do that. Could I?

Becca was silent for a moment. "The track meet tomorrow. We both have to be there. We can talk then."

"Just make sure it looks like we're not in this together," I said.

She laughed. "Wilderson, I can make it look like I find you as revolting as reading the school's mystery-meat recipe." She hung up.

"Okay," I muttered to the disconnected phone. I set it back down in its cradle and went to the kitchen for an ice-cream bar. Thinking about that mystery-meat recipe always left a bad taste in my mouth.

16

I LIKE SATURDAY TRACK
meets. I've had a few on weekdays, and though getting out of school early is awesome, it really puts a cramp in my work. Besides, I can get a good night's sleep before a Saturday meet.

Most of the time, anyway. This time I was up all night spinning the angles of the job around, looking at them from all sides. Mark and the key, Becca's motives, and most of all, my weird guilt. I couldn't stop thinking about the fire alarm and how Tate was being blamed for what I did. Did school justice work that fast when Becca wasn't involved? I couldn't think of a time when she had *not* been involved.

Every job I did, the job was all that mattered. But now, between Becca's comment at track practice and then finding out that Tate had been fingered for the fire alarm,

I was thinking about the consequences of what I had to do to finish the job. An anonymous note wouldn't save Tate now; the teachers had testified against her. Only an honest confession from the real culprit would. Becca would want me to do that.

Giving in to Becca and turning myself in would save Tate and others from getting hurt, but if I was in detention or suspended, I couldn't retrieve. What about all the other people who needed me when their lunch money got stolen or they left their science project in a locked room? Who would help them? This was what people were scared of, according to Becca: that I wouldn't be there to retrieve when they needed me.

But ever since Mark had gotten me to steal the key, this job had been my responsibility. It was up to me to make everything right, for as many people as I could. But how? My mind worked all night, and its noisy hammering kept the rest of me awake.

Saturday morning came too early, but I ate breakfast like nothing was wrong. At about ten Mom called me out to the car. As I piled in, I saw one of Mark's burly hit men—Sean—standing by our neighbor's mailbox. This time, though, he had a black eye.

"Is that a friend of yours?" Mom asked.

I shook my head. "I don't really know him."

I guess that wasn't completely true. After all, you can get to know a guy pretty well when his toes put a dent in your stomach. But that was need-to-know, and Mom really didn't need to know.

At the track meet Coach led us in our stretches and warm-ups, and then the team captain gave us our pep talk. He was an eighth grader, but a stand-up guy, unlike Mark. It was the captain's last meet as a Scottsville Middle School student, and he was in excellent form as he ranted about legacy and honor and beating the snot out of the other school's runners.

"Leave 'em in the dust!" he finished, and I admit I cheered just as loud as the rest of the team. Come on, it was a good speech!

The long-distance runners were up first, along with the field athletes in the middle of the track, then the sprinters like me. I sat on a shaky metal bench with my water bottle in hand; I had a long time to wait and watch as my teammates gave it their all in every area. Becca looked determined and scary as she threw the shot put.

"How can someone so tiny lift that much weight?" Case sat down beside me. Today he had no jersey, but his shorts had a Giants logo.

"You're not supposed to be here," I said. "Athletes only."

Case held up a card—forged, of course. "I'm equipment manager. I can go wherever I want. So can Hack."

"What's up?" Hack sat down beside Case. "Are we distracting you from your pre-race psych-up? Should I sing 'Eye of the Tiger'?" He seemed uncomfortable, as did Case.

"Please don't. Thanks for coming." I grinned, trying to figure out if my best friends still believed I was keeping them in the dark because I thought they weren't good enough to help me, or if they were just uncomfortable because my running shorts are *really* short. "I'm surprised you're here, Hack. Did your mom lift the grounding?"

"Not yet, but she's close. Supporting friends in their races is on the list of approved activities, and Mom said I could come as long as she does, too. She's over there in the stands." Hack waved, and his mom waved back at us.

"I take it she doesn't know you're not supposed to be over here," I said. "Or about last night. How late did you get to stay, Case?"

Case shrugged. "Later than I thought. Hack's mom called and said she had a date, so I got to stay until a little after ten."

"It got *wild*." Hack took my water bottle and chugged down a few deep gulps.

Case grabbed the bottle and handed it back to me. "Hack, 'wild' for you means playing RPGs while downing sodas."

"And there's something wrong with that?"

I laughed, and hesitated. "I'm sorry I missed it," I said. "Look, you really shouldn't be seen with me right now." I thought of Sean, waiting by my house. Other spies could be lurking in the crowd.

"Why not?"

"I can't say."

"More secrets?" Case looked annoyed. "J—"

"I know I'm running through your supply of trust, but I need you to pull out the reserves on this. I have things I need to work on, and I can't let you guys in."

"You are working something huge, aren't you?" Case asked. "Does it involve the fire drill? Or, should I say, the fire alarm?"

How did he know? I'd run out of lies. "Yeah."

Hack looked excited. "I knew it! I knew it! How'd you get Tate to agree to pull the alarm?"

"It was . . . easier than you'd think," I said. Very easy, since she didn't agree. "Don't worry; I'm figuring out a way to help her beat the rap."

After my sleepless night, I knew what I had to do. I just really, really didn't want to do it.

"So we're beating the rap now?" Hack looked thrilled. "Way to go, pushing the envelope and the limits and everything else that can be pushed."

"Including Becca Mills's buttons," Case added. "Watch out. Look at that smile." We looked at Becca, who was hurling another heavy metal ball. "She never looks that happy except when she's got enough to slam a guy with an in-school suspension."

Well, she had that. "That's just the high of breaking the laws of physics. But don't worry, I'll watch my back."

"We'll watch your back too," Case said. "I know you won't tell us anything, but that doesn't mean we won't help you if we can."

I looked at him and Hack. Could I tell them about Becca and what I'd agreed to do once the key job was done? It might be a good idea to get a second, non-Becca opinion on if my work was hurting people or helping them. But I knew what they would say, and I didn't want them knowing I'd gone to Becca, instead of them, when I needed help. They wouldn't like that.

"I'm in a lot of trouble on this one. Becca thinks what I do hurts people. If she's right, I don't want you to get caught in the whirlpool."

"I'm a great swimmer," Hack said cheerfully, which wasn't much comfort, since he's been in and out of detention/groundings since he was old enough to know what a firewall was.

Case put one glove to his mouth. "You're not . . . involved in this crime wave, are you?"

"No more involved than it takes to stop it. You should know that."

"Okay, okay, I do. I mean it. But you're not giving us a lot to go on, so I had to ask. From what I can tell, this crime wave has all the classic signs of a thief-on-thief turf war, and people *are* getting hurt in the crossfire. Innocent people who you're supposed to help. For once I think I'm with Becca on this."

That was *not* what I'd expected to hear from Case, but it made the knot inside me loosen a little. If Case agreed, then what I was going to do had to be the right thing. I was sure I'd be happy with it. When it was over.

"Agreeing with Becca? Let's not get crazy," Hack said.

Case grinned. "Yeah, that went a little too far, didn't it? She's kind of a psycho."

Nope, definitely not telling them. "Case, I'm not hurting anyone. I'm trying to stop whoever is. I promise. I've been working a job that's taken up all my time, but it's going to end soon."

"Then let us help you," Hack said. "Don't say no this time."

I gritted my teeth and shook my head. "Sorry, but it's another 'no.' Never mind that it's a dangerous job; I don't need a forger or a hacker." That much was true, at least, but it would take more to convince them. They'd weasel the truth out of me or, worse, they'd help behind my back. It was what I'd do for them.

Aha—I got it. "And Becca's onto me, but she doesn't know about your jobs at other schools. You don't want to get questioned by her, believe me. I don't want to see her use her tactics on you guys."

There you go: every word the truth. As far as I knew.

Hack nodded. "I believe *that*."

Case put his hand on Hack's shoulder. "Looks like it's going to be just you and me tonight. And J, I expect to hear every detail when this job is over."

"I'll replay it for you in high-definition. It'll be great. You'll laugh; you'll cry; you'll throw popcorn. Now get out of here before tiny Sam Spade starts chasing you too. I have to do some things."

"What's happening tonight?" Hack asked Case as they stood up.

"Oh, nothing more than two guys finishing their weekend homework because their good friend has to work."

"Very responsibly," Hack said, "which is a good thing,

because I get the feeling my mom is going to be very busy this evening. She may not be able to keep an eye on us."

Case lightly punched my elbow. "See you later, J."

"See ya."

As Case and Hack disappeared back into the crowd of spectators, I felt much better about our friendship. But I was worried that one of Mark's men had seen us talking and added my friends to his hit list. On the other hand, if they could see us, they might also be able to hear us, and our conversation would have made it clear Case and Hack weren't working with me. I'd made it sound like I was working alone, just as I'd told Mark.

I looked back at the crowd. Case and Hack leaned against the fence because the bleachers were full. On the bleachers I saw Mom and Dad with Rick, who looked surly because Mom says family sticks together and that means we support each other in our activities, even if we'd rather be eating pizza with friends. As I watched, Rick motioned at his eyes with two fingers and pointed them in the universal sign for *I'm watching you.* I followed Rick's fingers and saw black-eyed Sean. Beside him stood Hugo, with a new bruise on his chin.

Huh. I hadn't realized Rick cared. Considering how effectively he'd roughed up Mark's thugs, I guessed he'd been pulling his punches when he knocked me around.

"Wilderson! It's time." Coach Cread waved me down to the track.

I took the track. I *was* being watched, but my friends and my brother had my back. Time to run like nothing else mattered.

"Runners, take your mark," the ref said. "Get set."

I got set.

"GO!"

No need to go into details about running the race. Suffice it to say, I made our team captain proud and left the other guys in the dust. Maybe it was the adrenaline from knowing the bad guys were watching me, or maybe it was the support from the friends who were formerly mad at me (Hack yelled, "Burn 'em, J!" while I was running), but I sprinted better than I had in practice, and, believe it or not, I won my race.

I ran a couple other times that day, in a relay and a 200-meter dash, but that first race was the only one I won and the only one that mattered.

After I'd finished running and stretching and was resting on the side, Becca came up behind me and twisted my arm behind my back.

"All right, Wilderson, I have some questions for you," she growled. Loudly, I might add, and right in my ear. "Act like it hurts."

She had to add that last part, because it didn't. Hurt. At all. I scrunched up my eyes and groaned. "Let go, ow, that hurts!"

"I hope it does. Come on."

She dragged me in full sight of everyone—including my parents—away from the track and into a nook between the main school and the gym.

When she let go, I turned around. "So you know how to do that without hurting me?"

Becca grabbed the strap of her open gym bag, which was hanging loose from one shoulder, with both hands. "Have for a while."

"So all those other times, with the painful arm-twisting and kicking and shirt-grabbing . . . completely unnecessary."

She snorted. "It gave me peace of mind. Can't hurt you today, though. I need you in top physical form for phase three."

"Thanks." Once again this alliance had unforeseen perks. Next time Becca tried to kick me or twist my arm or slam me into a locker, I'd remind her of this moment. If there was another chance.

"Listen, Becca." I sighed and rubbed dried sweat from my forehead. "I've got something to tell you."

"What is it? Did Mark threaten you again?"

"No." I scratched my face harder. The words didn't come easily. "When it's over, and Mark gets caught, I'll let you turn me in." The last five words rushed out in a mumble.

"What was that?"

"I'll let you turn me in."

"Since when do I need you to 'let' me do anything?"

"Good point, but what I mean is . . . I'll confess to the charges. You won't need evidence."

Becca raised an eyebrow. "Am I supposed to take your word on it? What if you just want me to stop looking for evidence and then you'll deny everything at the last minute?"

She was right to be suspicious. "Tate. Tomboy Tate? She got blamed for the fire alarm."

"I know. I heard about it this morning. My friend Elena called me and told me everything."

"You were right: My actions did get someone hurt. I want to make it right."

For a moment that felt like it lasted three math classes, Becca eyed me. "If you get caught now," she said, "that's the end of it. Your work, your legacy, everything. The teachers will watch you too closely for you to start again."

"I know that." Boy, did I know it. Which was why Case and Hack couldn't know what I had planned.

Becca watched me, her eyes locking into mine. I didn't drop my gaze. She nodded, and smiled. "I'm glad you've come around. It's better this way, you know. Tate will go free with your confession, and you'll receive a reduced punishment for coming clean."

"I suppose I should feel better about that."

"I would, if I were you." Becca smiled. "I wonder what your parents thought of my performance back there?"

I felt the blood rush to my face. "My parents. Oh man, they saw you haul me off like that."

"I bet they think I have a crush on you."

I groaned. "I know. Why'd you have to do that?"

Becca shrugged. "It got the job done. Whatever your parents think, Mark's goons will only see our famous feud. You're right; he'll never imagine we're working together. But a good show doesn't hurt. By the way, I've got some important news for you."

"What?"

She looked at me, brow crinkled. "It's not good."

My skin prickled. "We knew it wouldn't be."

"I talked to Mark this morning, pretending I was looking for evidence against you. He got excited and told me one of his friends saw you on the phone with someone acting shady. Apparently, I should keep my eye out for an accomplice."

"So he *is* watching me at home." I'd hoped I was just being paranoid. "Wait. Was *I* the one acting shady, or was it the someone on the phone?"

Becca grinned. "You."

"Okay. Watch your grammar."

"Grow up. And in case you're getting any ideas, I am *not* your accomplice."

"Wouldn't want you if you'd have me."

"There's more. After school on Monday, Mark is going to tell the principal he saw you using the key. When he's asked for proof, he'll take McDuff to your locker, and when they get it open, they'll find a stash of stolen property."

"Placed there by him, using the master key. And then it will be my word against his, and the evidence will be in his favor." I clenched my fist so hard the nails bit into my palm.

"I should let you go down for it. It would solve everything."

"You won't because Mark will walk free. How do you know all this?"

"Mark told me this morning. Exactly what I just told you, and like you, I understood what he meant. Mark said he knew you kept your ill-gained goods in your locker, but he was waiting to tell the authorities because he wanted to be sure you really took the key before turning you in, but if what you say is true—"

"It is," I interrupted.

"Then Mark is just planning it as vengeance in case you attack again. Then he'll turn you in and you'll get burned for his crime while he walks free."

I jumped. "Who are you? The Becca I know would take every opportunity to remind me that this was *my* crime and *I* should be burned for it."

"Mark's the mastermind. You were just his pawn."

I put a hand on my chest. "Ouch. I thought *I* was the criminal mastermind."

"Maybe one of several. You'll burn for your own crimes; we've decided on that. But let's deal with Mark first. What do you want to do now that we know your head is on his chopping block?"

I had spent all night figuring that out. "We proceed as planned."

"Are you sure?" Becca said, peering at me. "That means Mark will go to the principal on Monday."

"I know. But so will you, right?"

"Not if we don't get Mark before then."

"Then we'll have to be ready for him Monday morning, early. Before he can do anything."

Becca smiled. She was cute when she wasn't trying to

destroy me. "We'll have him soon. And then our business is over."

"And so is mine." Why was I doing this? Oh, right, because I'd gotten in over my head, and this was the only way out. I nodded. "Okay. So, let's coordinate phase three. Does eleven o'clock tomorrow work for you?"

"Sounds good. Make sure you have an exit strategy this time, though."

"Don't worry. I'm ready for anything. But make sure he's not around when I'm working. Okay?"

Phase three was going to be the hardest part of this job, and once again, I was taking the worst of it while Becca played keep-away. I would need all my gear if I was going to stay out of trouble. Well, immediate trouble.

"Okay. Well, we have nothing more to say, do we?"

I shook my head.

Becca nodded. "Wait five minutes; then follow me. Don't let anyone see us together. Good run today. First place!"

I smiled. For a moment I really wished she'd say, *You know what, Wilderson? You provide a needed service. I'm going to save Tate, let you go, and stop chasing you.* But she had been chasing me for too long to let me go when she'd finally caught me.

And for one short moment I imagined what it would

have been like if she'd taken me up on my offer and took up retrieving instead of detective work. It would have been fun, I thought.

When she turned to leave, I started walking too. We collided as she stopped short, her gym bag smashing against me at waist level. "No, *you* wait five minutes, Wilderson," she said, annoyed.

"My bad. I heard it the other way around." I put my hands behind my back and waited the five minutes.

When I got back to the track, the long-distance runners were in the middle of their race. Since my races were done, I went to join the crowd of spectators.

Becca was talking to the coach. Her bag rested beside the fence, just far enough away from her to let me return the object I'd palmed earlier. I examined the item: a digital camera, small and silver. The same camera Becca carried everywhere, the one she had used to take pictures of Mark's stash.

I had to see. She'd tried to tape me confessing and she'd promised to find evidence to support her claim that I was behind the fire-alarm pull. Maybe she'd found that evidence and photographed it like she had Mark's stash. I needed to know if Becca had been ready to break our immunity deal long before I decided to come clean or only just before. It would tell me if I could trust her.

Also I wanted to know what she had on me besides my confession. If I was going down, I wanted to go down on my terms.

I flicked through the pictures on Becca's camera. A few of the races, a bunch of her friends at a pool, me in the girls' bathroom, the shots of Mark's stash, a few sneaky ones of my elbow vanishing around a corner (nice try, Nancy Drew), something that looked like it belonged to the mystery-meat case—wait. Go back.

I scrolled to the pictures of Mark's stash. All the stolen goods were heaped in the locker; Becca must have moved the trumpet case and the band jacket. And Case's forged hall passes sat on the pile in a place of incriminating prominence.

Had Becca noticed? She couldn't have, not yet. These pictures were meant to prove Mark's guilt, not Case's. But it wouldn't be long before she noticed and told the school authorities. They'd know the passes were fake, and they'd trace them back to Case. I couldn't let that happen. I deleted every picture of Mark's stash.

Feeling nauseous, I passed by Becca's bag and returned the camera. I hoped those pictures weren't the evidence needed to bring down Mark and make him return all the stolen items. They shouldn't be: I'd already returned everything from that day's stash, and if my plan went well, Mark would be stopped, no problem. I just hoped Becca wouldn't look at those pictures until after Monday.

"Jeremy! Congratulations!" I looked up. Mom and Dad were walking over, waving and smiling. I shouldered my gym bag, smiled back, and prepared for the praise I'd earned. It would be smooth sailing from here on out.

Or at least until tomorrow and phase three.

17

ON SUNDAY MORNING I GOT
up, ate breakfast, and immediately started preparations. Since I couldn't go over to Becca's, I'd have to trust she was doing the same. Not easy, since I still didn't trust her. But she wanted the key back, and we'd already agreed on how this arrangement would end. No reason to betray me when I'd agreed to turn myself in.

When I finished packing, my backpack contained the following: a change of clothes, three sticks of beef jerky, a length of rope, my grappling hook, my lockpick set, a pair of latex gloves, and a water bottle. Even if the worst should happen and Becca didn't manage to keep Mark away long enough, I'd have enough gear to get out of any situation.

Under my jacket I wore the Boy Scout uniform I'd bought at Goodwill last fall. It's part of being extra sneaky, as I was telling you earlier. Just wait until you see what I used the uniform for. It's kind of awesome.

Google Maps, crossed with Scottsville Middle's online student address book, had made it easy for me to take a scooter ride past Mark's house the night before. I'd have no trouble finding it again. I could take my scooter, but then I'd have to hide it, so I decided to walk.

I printed out a sheet of paper I'd prepared and left my house at about ten fifteen. I thought about taking the path through the woods behind my house—they gave me more cover, and it was usually pretty easy to spot a watcher among the monotone green and brown—but decided not to. Extra sneaky was the way to go on this job.

A few houses down I stopped and knocked on the door. No, it wasn't Mark's house. This performance was for any of his thuggish pets who may have had eyes on me.

The door opened and an elderly woman peered out. "Hi, ma'am," I said in my most upbeat voice. "I'm Jeremy. I live down the street. My troop is doing a service scavenger hunt. Do you have any work you need done, like taking out the trash or doing the dishes?"

"That's a nice activity. As a matter of fact, I need

someone to help me move a dresser. Think you can do it?"

"Yes, ma'am. When we're done, can you sign here that I completed my task?" I said, bringing out the sheet of paper I'd printed, which contained a list of possible jobs. "The first of us who finishes all of these gets ice cream."

She let me inside and I helped her move the dresser. It was heavy, but it was worth it for the legitimizing signature on the fake list. I repeated the deception until I reached Mark's house. By that time I had weeded one small flower bed, taken out two bags of trash, and carried a plate of cookies to someone's friend. Like a good little Scout. Too bad I wasn't one.

At last I reached Mark's house. He wouldn't be there, because Becca should have invited him to talk about the crime wave, or something. Anything to get him out of the way while I searched for the key. She was also supposed to case the joint a little bit. By the way, she and I had a little disagreement over the phrase "case the joint." She thought it sounded too thiefy.

The house looked similar to all the others in the neighborhood. A tree grew beside an upstairs window, and I saw a play place in the back with a swing and slide. Nice. How had Mark the Psychopath emerged from this picture-perfect home?

ALLISON K. HYMAS

At the top of the porch stairs sat a small planter with red flowers growing in it. Becca was supposed to leave me information about the house under it. I kicked it as I walked up the stairs, for the benefit of anyone watching me, and knelt quickly to catch it.

Nothing. No slip of paper, no code written in spilled dirt, nothing. My heart skipped. What had happened? Was Becca okay? And more important, why did I care if she was in trouble?

Maybe Becca hadn't come by yet, and if so, Mark might still be home. If he saw me, the game was up. But what if Becca *had* come by but hadn't been able to leave the note for me? I'd have to act now, before Mark came back.

What to do, what to do . . . I pressed my ear against the door. It sounded pretty quiet. Maybe I could chance it. Taking a deep breath and hoping I hadn't run out of luck, I knocked. A few minutes later a guy opened the door.

"Yeah?" This guy looked about high school age, maybe older, and annoyed at me for interrupting him. Mark's brother.

Working a retrieval job takes skill, hard work, and occasionally a bit of luck. This was an example of the kind of luck I mean. Big brothers are way easier to work with than parents or the mark itself.

"Look, I'm not buying any popcorn," he said. He started to close the door.

I grabbed the door, stopping it. "Nothing like that," I said, making my voice cheerful and Scout-like. "Though I hope I can count on you later when we do that fund-raiser. No, today I'm doing a service activity for my troop and I was wondering if there was anything around the house you would like me to do."

"Not interested."

"Come on, please? If I do more jobs than anyone else, I get ice cream. Are you sure I can't help out? Look," I said, pushing my checklist at him. "I can vacuum your carpets, or wash windows, or clean your room—"

Something in there got his attention. He pushed the door open a little wider and said, "Did you say vacuum?"

"I did. Would you like me to do that?"

The guy smiled. As it turned out, vacuuming the upstairs was his chore for the weekend and he'd put it off. It was good luck that I'd come around offering to do his work for him.

Or maybe it wasn't just luck. Becca wasn't the only one who had (or should have) cased this house. As I said earlier, I'd come here the night before, which was how I'd been able to recognize Mark's house on sight. I just couldn't get inside, so she'd had to do that for me.

In any case, as I passed by I'd had to fake a spill on my scooter because I'd heard Mark's mom start to nag his brother—whose name I never got—about vacuuming before the weekend was over. If he was anything like my brother, I knew that he'd do it around midnight Sunday night.

Cons work best when you offer the mark something they want, while asking for something acceptable but a little dishonest in return. In the best-case scenario this guy would never learn I was using him, and if everything went south, he wouldn't say a word about my involvement because he shouldn't have farmed out his chores in the first place.

It was the same thing that kept me safe from Mark telling anyone I'd retrieved his stash. If he wasn't supposed to have it in the first place, he couldn't exactly run crying to Principal McDuff, or even Becca. All Becca had to go on was my confession. Ugh. I couldn't believe I was going to give it to her. Was it too late to back out? Yeah, probably.

Anyway, the con worked; I was in. Mark's brother showed me the closet with the vacuum cleaner and helped me carry it upstairs. He said politely, "Let me know if you need any help," but his heart wasn't in it.

"I'll be fine," I said, acting as cheerful as ever. "I can

let myself out when I'm done, if you want. Just sign my list right now."

Mark's brother happily did so. "Oh," he said, handing the list back to me. "I should go tell her you're here too."

"Her?"

"Just a friend of my brother's. She's putting together some kind of surprise in his room." Mark's brother smiled, but he didn't say anything. Clearly he thought that this girl (three guesses, who do you think it was?) *like*-liked his brother, but that I was too young to understand.

I'm short, not a baby.

And I understood perfectly. "How about I go up and tell her I'm here? Just so she doesn't think her surprise is ruined?"

"Sure. It's the one on the end, that way." Mark's brother pointed and then went back to whatever he was doing before I interrupted him. Video games, probably. Fun, but who needs games when you live the adventure?

I went upstairs, glancing into the other rooms as I went, checking to make sure no one but the brother was home. Far right was the parents' room; it had a double bed and its own bathroom. In the middle of the hall was a room filled with posters of bands and an electric guitar in the corner. It smelled like the inside of Rick's sneakers. The older brother's. That left the one on the end. Mark's room.

Time to make an entrance. I plugged the vacuum in and turned it on, right outside Mark's room. Then I threw open the door. Over by the desk Becca jumped, dropping the stack of papers she had in her arms.

I helped her gather them. "I had no idea you were the sneaking-and-entering type."

"I'm a detective. It's part of the job description." She looked me over. "Nice uniform."

"Thanks, it's vintage. I thought keeping the mark away from the area while your partner worked was also part of the job description."

"First off, I'm not your partner." Becca took the papers from me and set them on Mark's desk. Where they belonged, I assumed. She was wearing disposable gloves, and she snapped one threateningly at me. "Second, I can't keep being the distraction. He'll notice that you always search his stuff while I'm chatting him up. Besides, I have to find Mark's stash."

"It would have been great if you could have brought me in on your change of plans here. I could have helped. How did you get Mark out of the house?"

"Who said I did?"

I gave her a look, and she shrugged. "I called him and told him to meet me in the park by the art museum. I gave him reasons why I might have to run suddenly, so when he realizes I'm not there, he won't get suspicious."

"That doesn't leave you much time, either. He'll come back as soon as he knows you're not going to show."

"I don't need much time."

I nodded. "It doesn't take too long to leave your crush a token of your affection. What is Mark's brother going to think when you don't actually leave kiss-stained letters on Mark's bed?"

Becca opened a drawer and picked through it with the end of a pencil. "I'm going to find something that proves he doesn't like me back, and leave angry."

"He'll tell Mark about it later. Trust me. I have a brother. I know."

"It will be too late then."

"Why is it that when you lie and sneak around, it's good detective work, but when I do it, it's thieving?"

"Are you here to help me or not?"

"I'm here for the key. You're after the stash." But I nodded. "Let me just prepare *my* cover."

I went back to the hall and pushed the vacuum back

and forth down the hall. That way the vacuum would leave tracks in the carpet that would cover my alibi with the brother. Hallway finished, I pulled the vacuum in front of Mark's room and let it run.

"Pretending to like Mark," I muttered as I scanned the room for places Mark might have hidden the key. "You're really sacrificing a lot for this case."

"I'm not the only one." Becca stared at me. We turned away from each other at the same time. Didn't need things to get weird.

Okay, get to work. Phase three. Mark wouldn't want that key hidden anywhere he couldn't get to it in a hurry, so his was the only room in the house it could be in. Time to knock it over.

"We'll have to keep this short," I told Becca. "Under five minutes."

"*You* do. I have a little more time."

"Whatever." I pulled the latex gloves out of my backpack and put them on. I didn't think Mark would search for fingerprints, but I couldn't let anything slip out of my grasp and break.

In hiding the key, Mark needed to think like a thief. He also needed to try to outsmart me, or the version of me he thought he knew. Too bad for him, I was a better retrieval specialist than he was a thief *and* I was experienced at outsmarting people smarter than him. Come to think of it, I owed Becca for that.

The first place I checked was the drawer on the bedside table. Nope, no key there. Anyway, it was too obvious a hiding place.

As I pulled the drawer out and held it up to check that he hadn't taped the key to the bottom, Becca opened the closet and peeled back a layer of clothes. "Are all guys this gross?"

I looked over. "Looks fine to me."

Becca sniffed and went back to work.

The next place I searched was the bottom of Mark's clothes drawers. I know I make my work seem glamorous, but I can tell you that rifling through layers of an eighth grader's underwear is anything but. Mark *was* a little more disgusting than the average guy. And on top of that, I didn't find the key.

My time was running out. "Move over, Becca." I checked inside the shoes in his closet before making sure all the books on his shelf were real and not cleverly disguised boxes. I even examined the light fixtures. Nothing.

If I waited much longer, the brother was going to wonder why it was taking me so long. I stood there confused, looking around the room. If I were a thief, a real thief, and I needed to hide something from a better thief, where I would I put it?

My eyes rested on the bed. No way. No *way* would he hide the treasured master key in the most obvious place in his room. But then again, he would guess I'd think it was too obvious to search.

I dropped to my stomach and peered under the bed.

Becca looked over from the closet, where she was checking the top shelf. "Really? That's too obvious."

"Maybe it's just obvious enough." Jackpot. A black metal box sat under his bed. I reached under and pulled it out.

"No way." Becca abandoned the closet and knelt beside me on the floor. She crouched and checked under the bed. "I wonder if his stash could be in here too."

"Maybe some of it's in this box with the key."

I tried to open the box.

It, of course, was locked. Thank goodness I had my handy-dandy lockpick set with me. It might leave scratches on the lock, but Mark wouldn't notice them until it was too late. After examining the lock, I pulled out the wires best suited for its width and complexity.

"You brought those?" Becca had some lint in her hair. I decided my life wasn't worth telling her that.

"Aren't you glad I did?" A minute later I heard a faint

click. "Got it." I threw the lid up. We both looked inside and gasped.

"There's too much cash in there," Becca said as she pulled wads of money out.

I took a stack too, just to look at it. Fives, tens, twenties . . . it made the Andrew Jackson he'd offered me look like chump change. I thought about the thug kids Mark had hired. It looked like he'd already begun to sell the stolen goods. That wasn't good.

Becca eyed the money in my hands. "No."

I dropped the cash. "Don't worry. I'm not even tempted."

For the record, I wasn't. The money was dirty, made from selling the belongings of other people. As much as I wanted Mark to hurt for his crime, I didn't want any part of his earnings.

Gingerly, like I was handling a live bomb, I set the bills inside and looked for any glint of metal with a big black *X* on it. After a thorough search I had to admit it: no master key.

"Dang it!"

"Not here?" Becca smirked, and opened her mouth to verbally abuse me further. But she stopped when we both heard, over the whine of the vacuum, a door open and close downstairs.

Dang it twice. "Time's up." I closed the lid of the box

and slid it back under the bed; there wasn't enough time to relock it.

Becca's eyes widened in fear. "He can't catch me here. He'll know I suspect him."

"Never mind the poking around a room that's not yours."

She paled. "Mom will kill me."

"I don't want to get caught either. Hold on."

I opened the door and pulled the vacuum's plug out of the wall. The sound died, letting me hear the conversation downstairs.

"Aren't you supposed to be vacuuming?" Mark was home!

"Aren't you supposed to be out with a friend?" his brother replied.

"We've got to go." I wound up the cord on the vacuum as fast as I could and quietly opened the door. Mark and his brother were downstairs, but Mark was facing away from me. I closed the door quietly.

"Mark's down in front of the door. His brother's going to tell him enough to make him suspicious. We don't have long."

"Got some brilliant escape plan?" Becca started to take off her gloves.

"Leave those on. You might need them. And shouldn't

a master detective know how to get out of scrapes?"

"Normally I can talk my way out of them. I don't think that will work on Mark."

"It won't."

"I know. So? Plan?"

"Give me a minute." I looked around the room, weighing my options. They were disappointingly light.

Okay. I couldn't go downstairs or Mark would see me. The room didn't have many hiding places big enough for two people, and Mark would check those places first. We had to get out of the room. Me and Becca both. Or we'd blow the whole con.

I went to the window. The tree I'd seen earlier wasn't far from the glass. The nearest branch hung about ten feet away, give or take two feet. Yes. It was my only bet. Mine *and* Becca's. She wasn't going to like this.

Becca joined me at the window. When she saw the tree, she shook her head. "No way."

"It's our only chance. Mark's probably already on his way up." I slid off my backpack and pulled out my grappling hook and rope. I tied the rope to the hook. "Open the window."

"You're insane. I'm not doing this. We'll fall and break our necks."

"You sound like my mom."

My heart raced: I had never used the grappling hook before. I'd practiced with it in my yard, but when you're in the middle of a job and jumping out of a second-story window is your only way out, no preparation is really enough.

Becca opened the window. Now for the tricky part. I judged the angle I'd need to throw the grappling hook to snare the branch. My hook was made of the remains of a metal lamp Mom used to have before it broke. Four curlicues made up the base, and above those was a thick stalk with a hole I'd painstakingly made with Dad's power-drill for the rope. When the knot was tied tight, the hook could hold my weight; I'd tried it. But could it also hold Becca's?

No time to think. I threw the hook out and over the tree branch, letting its weight wrap it around the branch. One of the curlicues caught the rope, securing it.

"Perfect," I whispered. "Climb on my back."

"What?"

"I don't have time to give you a lesson in grappling-hook safety. Climb on my back and hold on tight." I put my backpack on backward, on my chest.

Becca muttered angrily, but she climbed on. She gripped me so tight I thought I'd lose feeling in my arms in ten seconds and pass out in twenty, but at least it made her easier to carry.

"So, uh . . ." I let my hands hover in the air. I wanted to shift her higher but couldn't think of a way to do it that wasn't awkward. "How about we don't tell anyone about this, okay?"

"I've already forgotten what we're doing."

"Okay. Me too." She smelled good, like raspberries and something else. Chocolate, maybe?

I heard Mark's voice and steps on the stairs. My heart jumped. Time to get out of there, or everything would be ruined.

Focus. I tied the other end of the rope around my waist. I sat on the windowsill, sighing as I looked at the twenty-foot drop below me, a drop that would break my legs if the grappling hook failed.

Don't look down, I told myself, but my knees went weak anyway. Then, eyes closed and face turned in against my shoulder, I slid down and out the window.

My hands burned with pain as the rope tried to slip from my grip. The latex gloves helped, but they tore quickly. Becca's weight fizzled my calculations and dragged me down to the grass below. Gritting my teeth, I tightened my hold, and the burn turned to a joyful thrill in my stomach as I swung through the air toward the tree.

Becca gasped, and I opened my eyes to the trunk rushing at me. I kicked out, stopping my swing with my feet. Using the rope, I pulled Becca and myself into the tree's branches on the side of the tree away from the house. Then I pulled the rope up so that no one would suspect anyone was hiding in the branches.

The tree was leafy, an adequate hiding place until the coast was clear. I looked up at the open window and decided not to worry about it; as long as Mark couldn't prove we'd been in his room, it didn't hurt to remind him he wasn't clear yet.

Mark came to the window and looked outside. Becca and I shrank back into the shadows. Mark frowned and closed the window. After he didn't return, I breathed easier.

"I did it!" I gasped. "It worked, it really worked."

"You mean you weren't sure?" Becca sounded annoyed.

"Your presence on Flight One-Twenty from Mark's bedroom wasn't expected."

Becca pushed me, hard enough to unbalance me but not knock me out of the tree. "That was stupid and dangerous."

"And you loved it."

"No, I didn't."

But she had. Her eyes shone, and although she kept

trying to frown at me, a wild smile twisted the corners of her mouth. I recognized that smile: I'd gotten it the first time I did a risky job. The thrill of the heist had gotten to her.

I grinned. "It's not all bad, what I do, right?"

Becca was quiet. She looked at Mark's window and let the smile slide out. "The things you can do . . . maybe they are needed. Sometimes. That's all I'm saying."

Before I could ask her to please discuss that response a little more, Becca took off her gloves and waved them at the ground. "Elevator or stairs?"

"Give it a minute. Wait for Mark to—" Mark ran out of his house, looked around his yard, and then tore off through the neighborhood. "See, that wasn't so bad."

"Get chased often?"

"You'd be surprised." I untied the rope from my waist and handed it to Becca. "Ladies first."

Phase three was complete. I held the rope steady while Becca climbed down—which hurt a lot; my hands were still raw from the swing, and I found myself supporting her weight more than I expected. But I kept it together, and she made it safely down. She smiled and saluted me, and then left.

I gripped the rope and swung from the tree to the ground. I had to escape before Mark realized I was there. The landing wasn't too rough, and it only took a little maneuvering to loosen the hook free from the tree branch.

Then I raced back home. After Monday the job would be done, and after that . . . so would I. At least I'd gotten to use my grappling hook. Even with Becca choking me, it had been a blast.

THE NEXT MORNING I GOT

ready and left for school early with my mom, feeling nervous like I hadn't felt in months. Even though the job was almost done and Mark's crime spree was in its endgame, I was still in danger. Mark knew that I had been inside his house, and he wouldn't be happy. They say that a trapped animal is the most dangerous, and I had trapped him. He'd be looking for me.

Not to mention, Monday was my last morning of freedom. After Mark got a desk in detention, it was my turn. Tate would go free and my conscience would be clear, but that meant no more retrieving. Ever.

I sighed. And, for this last day of my last job, I didn't have any of my gear with me. Not even my lockpick set. Becca had been very clear about that.

"If you bring any of your thieving tools, it will be

worse for you," she'd told me over the phone the night before as we finalized our plan. "That's a promise."

Like I didn't know how she felt about me. But seriously, after all we'd been through, she didn't trust me? I'd done everything right while she kept throwing me under the bus. My quick band-room retrieval and fire-alarm pull were beside the point. We had a professional relationship now. I'd fix my mistake and save Tate, and she'd take down the two thieves responsible for all the trouble.

Well, it was nice while it lasted.

Mom dropped me off in front of the school before going to park in the teachers' lot, and as soon as she pulled away, Mark's thugs materialized. They didn't move, but I felt their eyes follow me into school.

Act natural, I told myself. Easier said than done. I missed the weight of my lockpick set in my pocket. Not having it severely limited my escape avenues. I had to rely on Becca to show up with the teachers. Otherwise I was doomed.

Hugo and Sean followed me, not too subtly, as I wandered the empty halls. I had to buy some time for Becca to get to school and round up the teachers. How long would I be able to go before the guys behind me got impatient?

I passed the cafeteria, and then I circled around and passed it again. The clocks displayed the minutes changing, so slowly that I wondered if they were broken. Sean and Hugo were still behind me.

The empty hallways echoed with our steps. For a while, as I turned down the sixth-grade hall for the third time, the steps behind me were slow, measured. Then I heard them speed up, sneakers slapping against the hard floor as Mark's thugs decided they were done chasing me in circles.

"Oh, great!" I started running. It was too early for Becca to have arrived at school! I needed to keep stalling.

I looked behind me. Sean and Hugo pounded the linoleum, getting closer and closer.

But sprinters they were not. Their huge bulk weighed them down, while my small size and training let me move with efficiency and agility. The distance between us grew, and I turned corner after corner, trying to get more of a lead. I couldn't shake them, not with the way our steps echoed in the halls. But if I could get far enough away, I could hide.

In the next hall there'd be the library. It was where I always went when I arrived early with Mom and didn't have a job. I'd read or mess around on a computer until other kids started showing up. Ms. Gimbel, the librarian, was always there early, and Sean and Hugo wouldn't dare try anything while she was there. I could wait for Becca to arrive in safety.

Slowing just enough to avoid making a scene, I rushed through the library doors. The place was empty. Ms. Gimbel must have been taking coffee in the teachers' lounge, because the library was a graveyard, each book a tombstone. Or maybe it just seemed that way to me.

Standing out in the open wasn't doing me any favors. I crossed the room into the shelves, getting cover just as Sean and Hugo entered the library. As I watched through a narrow gap between two dictionaries, the thugs sat down in worn wooden chairs right next to the door. My only escape, under surveillance. I shrank back into the shelves.

I wandered into the mystery section and tried to guess which fictional detectives Becca most admired. Which ones liked hanging suspects upside down from balconies? That sounded right up her alley.

I looked back out at Hugo and Sean. Hugo had pulled out a cell phone, and his thumbs flew over the keys. Mark would be here soon. How long had it been? Had Becca made it to school yet? Had she gotten the teachers? Where was Ms. Gimbel? And, for that matter, where was Mark?

The library door creaked open and shut with a whoosh of air. The silence felt like wet concrete, wrapping around me, squeezing the air out of my lungs. I wandered back down the length of the mystery novels, running my finger along the spines. If Becca didn't show up . . .

"Hello, Wilderson," a smug voice said.

I turned away from the shelf and stared into Mark's icy eyes. "Hey, Mark. How was your weekend? Mine was great. Got a nice tour of your room."

Mark smirked. "Coming to my house was a big mistake. You didn't get the key, did you?"

I sighed, the picture of defeat. "No."

Mark nodded, and Hugo and Sean stepped to his sides, blocking my escape route. *Come on, Becca.*

"I'm not giving up," I said, "in case you were wondering."

"It doesn't matter if you give up or not. Your poking around ends today. As soon as school is over." He smiled. "Maybe earlier, if I get the chance. How's lunchtime sound?"

I shook my head. "Stop trying to act all mysterious. I know you're going to put a bunch of the less-valuable stolen stuff in my locker and then go running to Principal McDuff. Your evidence against my word, and I'll get pinned for the thefts."

I tried to walk away, but Sean placed an arm in my way and Hugo grabbed my shoulder. The bruised one, I might add. I turned back and leaned against the shelves, arms folded.

Mark put one arm on either side of me, trapping me there. "What's the matter, Wilderson? Sad that it's all over?"

"Sad that a simple frame job is the only thing you could come up with to end my career. You didn't think it through. Sure, I'll get in trouble. I'm picturing detention plus community service. But when the key never turns up, they'll take another look at *my* story and come looking for you." I rolled my eyes. "Small potatoes, Mark. That's all you are."

Mark's eyes bugged out of his skinny face. "Small potatoes?"

"Tater tots."

Mark's voice got low, and his hands on either side of me gripped the shelves until the knuckles turned white. "*I'm* small-time? *I* don't have what it takes? I've pulled off the greatest crime wave in Scottsville Middle's history without leaving a trace of evidence. Everyone's afraid of me; I'm untouchable now. And then there's you. You made a mess when you went through my backpack, my locker, and my room. Yes, I know you were there." His voice grew louder and louder, almost to a shriek. "Papers everywhere, books out of place. Oh, and leaving that snarky note on the twenty-dollar bill in my locker? You might as well have put up a sign saying, 'Jeremy Wilderson was here'!"

The library door creaked, and several pairs of footsteps shuffled through. One pattern—a sharp, determined pace—was familiar. My heartbeat slowed. Finally. Took her long enough, but she came through.

"Well, yeah," I said. "That was kind of the point. How else could I scare you enough?"

Mark drew back. "Enough for what?"

I shrugged. "If I found the key, it would have been great. But then you wouldn't have paid your debt to society. I didn't need to find the key. I just needed to make sure the key was on *you*."

"Wh-what?"

I smiled. "Fear works both ways, man."

"Mark Chandler?"

The eighth-grade wannabe thief looked over and saw Principal McDuff standing where Sean used to be. The thugs—showing the strong sense of self-preservation such meatheads tend to have in place of their common sense and sense of humor—had fled the scene.

Becca hung a little behind the principal, grinning.

Next to her was Natalie, our guidance counselor and the adviser to the peer mediators.

"Mark," Principal McDuff said, "will you come with me, please? Into the hallway."

"But . . . he . . . did you hear . . . ?"

"Now."

Mark knew the game was up. I could see it in the way the blood drained from his face. But he had one move left up his sleeve. Grabbing my arm, he said, "This is the guy. This is the guy who took the key. He stole everything. I found him for you."

I didn't say it was a *good* move.

Becca snorted and turned it into a cough. Principal McDuff frowned. "Is that so?"

Mark nodded. "He did everything. He has the key."

Principal McDuff glanced at Becca, who shook her head. Then the principal nodded at me. "Turn out your pockets," he said to me.

Shaking Mark loose, I did so. A bit of lint fell out, instead of the lockpick set I usually carried. *Good call, Becca.* I wondered if she'd guessed Mark would try to throw the blame on me.

Principal McDuff turned to Mark. "Now it's your turn."

"But I didn't do it!"

"If you didn't do it, you have nothing to fear,"

Guidance Counselor Natalie said. "Now do what your principal says."

Mark put his hands in his pockets and glared at me. "That kid is a thief. He's been stealing things all year. Everyone knows it. You're just going to let a crook like that go?"

"Jeremy's innocent," Becca said. "What about you?"

"Thanks for that endorsement," I said. "Really means a lot."

"Mark," Principal McDuff said. "If you please."

"But—"

Principal McDuff looked at him sternly. The silence felt as thick and heavy as a wool sweater. Just as uncomfortable, too.

Mark had nowhere to turn. He reached into his pocket and pulled out the master key.

Principal McDuff put out his hand and Mark dropped the key in his palm. "I'm very disappointed in you, Mark," the principal said.

"But Jeremy's the one who stole it! Ask him."

"How can that be?" Becca said. "You had it. Why would a thief give you a key that can open every locker in the school when he could keep it and use it himself?"

Again, thank you, Becca.

Principal McDuff leveled Mark with a stern look

somewhere between *disapproval* and *silently furious*. "I think you should come with me. We have to call your parents."

The principal turned and left, Mark following in his wake. Natalie stayed behind a moment. "Thank you, Becca."

"Happy to help," Becca said.

"Will you give your statement? It could help us understand how best to deal with Mark."

"Soon," Becca said. "Let me just finish up here."

The guidance counselor nodded.

"Natalie?" Principal McDuff called. He was waiting by the door with Mark. "I'd like you to be there when we call his parents."

"I look forward to hearing your side of the story," Natalie said to Becca. She smiled at me and left.

The library had huge windows overlooking the hallway. I guess that was supposed to be enticing to us students, showing us all the pretty books we could read, but all they ever did was make me think how easy it would be for someone to smash the glass and run off with the books. Not me, of course, but someone.

But now the windows were my friend. They gave me a great view of Mark being led away in handcuffs.

Well, there were no handcuffs, obviously, but you know what I mean.

"Yes!" I allowed myself a discreet double fist pump. Becca smiled.

She put out a hand, and I slapped it, just as Mark looked through the window back at me. His face turned from misery to shock and then anger as he saw who my partner had been this whole time. But what could he do?

"I have to hand it to you. That was a great plan," Becca said.

"He could have hidden it anywhere," I said. "But if he thought I was after him—"

"That you were looking for the key—"

"He'd keep it close. He knows I'm better at this than him. All I had to do was eliminate the easy places and force him to keep it in his pocket."

Becca leaned against the shelf. "And all *I* had to do was bring in the authorities as soon as he was on school grounds." She laughed. "His whole plan to frame you backfired. He'd need the key on hand to get into your locker, and he'll have all the stolen goods in his own locker right now, waiting to be moved."

"It's like he set himself up!" I laughed. It felt *great* to be off the hook. Well, off the hook with Mark. With Becca I had unfinished business.

"Okay, I guess it's my turn."

Becca eyed me. "Your turn for what?"

"You know, our deal. After Mark was taken care of, it was my turn." Becca didn't move or speak, so I continued. "Remember? Tate's still in trouble. How much do you need to make sure she gets off free? I can give you everything. On Friday I—"

"Stop." Becca's hand was on my mouth. When had that happened? "Tate's free."

It was a trap. It had to be. "What?" I mumbled through her fingers.

"This morning, new evidence appeared that made it clear that Tate wasn't responsible for the fire alarm. Her parents were told the truth, and apologies were made all over the place. She's fine."

"Oh." A sudden, scary thought gripped me. "Then who do they think did it?" I didn't want another innocent person blamed for what I did.

"You."

"Then why didn't Principal McDuff take me down to the office too?"

"I'm sure he'll call you down later to get your statement. But right now you're a lower priority because he's dealing with Mark. Plus, everyone understands *why* you did it."

To rifle through someone else's belongings undisturbed? I was confused.

Becca pulled a plastic bag out of her backpack. Inside was a charred piece of what looked like a dishrag. "I went looking for evidence, in case your confession turned out to be a ploy. I found this. Nineteen student witnesses and one teacher say you did run to pull the fire alarm, but only because there was a grease fire in the cafeteria. Goodness knows there's enough grease there to burn down a National Forest. So I guess you're off the hook for that. Unless you started the fire?"

"No, not me. Wow." A real fire the day I pulled the alarm? People vouching for me?

"Yeah. Weird coincidence, but it worked out well for you. I guess you *are* untouchable."

I pointed at the burned towel. "Can I keep that?"

She handed it over. "Sure. It's not like it's part of an investigation."

I turned the bag over in my hands, examining it. "What about the other stuff? When are you going to take me in for that?"

Becca frowned and touched her chin. "You know, I really should. I can't let it get out that I let *the* Jeremy Wilderson get away with crimes he committed on my watch."

I groaned. There it was. "You're a PI," I said. "You have a reputation to uphold."

"Sure." Becca paused, then smiled. "And so do you. Can you imagine the riots I'd have to deal with if you weren't on the job anymore? That many kids in need, scared because you're not there to help them . . . A girl can only manage so much."

"I'm sure you'd find a way." I waved the towel around. "Why are you doing this? I thought you wanted me stopped so I couldn't hurt anyone. I was ready to let you."

Becca shrugged. "Maybe I just don't want to leave some innocent kid hanging, say, when she's stuck on the second floor and needs to escape fast."

Um, what was that? I gaped at Becca, who turned away from me. I swear, though, she was smiling.

"I knew you liked the grappling hook."

She looked over her shoulder. "You have skills. I'm ready to ignore your past crimes if you use those skills to help people in need. It's not like I ever found evidence anyway."

"What do you mean?"

Becca shrugged. "There's . . . there's a place for you. But it had better be an honest place. I won't ignore future crimes. Consider this your warning: You're out of the thief business."

Yeah, like that was going to happen. Not as long as

I could help people and build my fame. I'd just be more careful about who I took jobs from and who could get caught in the crossfire if there was trouble.

"What about Mark?" I asked.

"Oh, that. They'll search his locker. They'll find the stolen goods he was going to put in your locker, and he'll get punished. I doubt leaving for high school will wipe his slate clean. This will follow him for a while. At least everyone's going to get their stuff back."

"Not everyone. Remember all that cash in his box? I'd bet a slice of three-layer chocolate-mousse cake that Mark's already sold some of his ill-gotten gains." I thought of Sean and Hugo. "How else could he hire thugs?"

"That's true. You've never . . . have you?"

"What, me? Fence stolen property? Of course not! I'd have to steal something to do that."

"Whatever. Know anyone I should look into?"

I thought. "I might know a few fences you could talk to. Better yet, let me talk to them. They trust me."

"Because you were a thief?"

"A retrieval specialist, but actually it's because I've helped them out once or twice before."

Becca shook her head but smiled. "'Retrieval specialist.' Okay. This once, at least. You know, with your knowledge about this school's underground, you'd make a formidable detective. It's a positive way for you to keep using those talents."

Detective work . . . nah, not my style. Too many rules. "I'll keep that in mind. But, for what it's worth, you'd make a decent retrieval specialist, too."

"Not sure what I think of that, but I guess it's a compliment." Becca sighed. "I'm going to be pretty busy trying to track down everything Mark sold."

"I always could get it back by . . . other means."

"No. Absolutely not. No more thieving, Jeremy. You're honest now. Work one more job, and I swear, I will bring you down so fast your ears will pop." She rummaged in her backpack. "But don't worry about me. Look. I've got what I need to start." Her hand emerged, carrying her slim camera.

Oh no. "Wait, let me explain—"

She clicked through the saved files, interrupting me. "Where are the photos? The shots of Mark's stash?"

"Gone. But it's okay. You don't need them. I already returned everything that was in that stash."

She shook the camera at me. "When did you do it? When did you erase the pictures?"

"I borrowed the camera at the race. I found the pictures and I guess I pressed the wrong button and deleted them." It sounded lame even to me, but I couldn't tell her the truth and let Case get in trouble.

But Becca didn't call me out on my bad lie. Her voice quiet, she said, "You stole from me?"

"Borrowed. I put the camera back. It's just missing a couple of pictures you don't need." I smiled, trying to lose the tension that had sparked up between us. "Good thing you have a retrieval specialist on your side."

Becca looked at the camera and then up at me. The expression on her face was strange. I couldn't tell if she was about to laugh or throw me out of one of the library's huge windows. "Oh no," she said, her lips forming a wicked smile. "No, no, no. Not a retrieval specialist, not a chance. You are a *thief*, Wilderson."

"Wait, I thought I got immunity for everything I did before right now. I borrowed the camera before the job was done. It's like sneaking into Mark's house."

Becca shoved the camera in her pocket and grabbed my shirt. Once more I found myself trapped against the mystery books.

"This is entirely different," she hissed in my ear. "You went through my things and you took my camera while we were supposed to be partners. Even worse, those pictures were evidence, and you took them from me. You *stole* from *me*."

Well, at least Case will be okay, I thought. *No heat for the forged hall passes, whatever happens to me.*

"I can't bring you in for stealing the master key," Becca said, making me sag with relief. "That would only get Mark out of the trouble he deserves. Without your confession—which I'm sure you won't give now—I can't bust you for anything. Twenty people swear you pulled the fire alarm because you were trying to be helpful. It's true; I can't do anything to you. But I will be watching you, Wilderson. I will stop your illegal activities."

"What happened to people needing my skills?"

"Now that I think about it, I'm sure they can manage without you. You do more harm than good, and when I find enough evidence, I'll prove it to everyone."

"After everything that happened, you still don't understand that I don't leave evidence unless I want to."

"Trust me, I will find it. I know what to look for now. I've never been more motivated." She grinned, evil to the core, and walked away with a toss of her hair. "Watch your step."

I waved good-bye, but she never looked back.

I watched her walk past the big windows toward the sixth-grade hallway. Good riddance. I was free to work alone again, no nasty gumshoe breathing down my neck.

But as pleased as I was to have my life back, I felt a twinge of loss. Even with all the insults and mistrust and apparent hatred, it had been fun working with Becca. She was clever and tricky; plus, the job had been *exciting*. Knowing that I would never have another job like that, well, it made me feel as though the cafeteria had stopped having Pizza Friday.

Somehow, being left unscathed had never felt so painful. I decided it was lingering guilt for almost getting someone else in trouble for pulling the fire alarm.

Speaking of that . . . I examined the burned rag in the plastic bag. It looked so right, from the blackened cloth to the grease that soaked the rest of the rag. Either there really had been a grease fire in the cafeteria or . . .

Or I had a friend with enough professional pride to care whether a rag looked like it had burned in a campfire or a grease fire.

Just then Case and Hack walked into the library, arguing. Speak of the devil.

As I watched, Hack sat down at a computer and Case, in a Seahawks T-shirt with a pencil behind his ear, said, "You're going to get suspended."

"Will not. This isn't even illegal." Hack's hair looked like he'd slept upside down at a power plant, evidence that the grounding was officially off.

"I doubt that. I really do."

"People lie online all the time."

"This isn't lying. This is forgery."

"Which is why I brought you along."

I smiled and crept—like a cat or a thief—to where my friends sat by the computer. "New job?" I said, leaning in over their heads.

They jumped. Hack recovered quickly. "Not really. I just had this idea and I thought I could use it to extend my client base. His, too," he said, pointing to Case.

"How is your job going?" Case asked.

"Oh, the job you know nothing about? Great. I almost got in serious trouble, but it seems someone convinced twenty people that not only did they see me pull the fire alarm, but I did it with good intentions. And then there's this." I handed Case the burned rag.

He held the bag up to the light. "Decent work. Whoever did this is an adequate forger."

"Who says it didn't come from a real, honest fire?" I grinned. "Thanks, guys."

"Save your thanks. It wasn't us." Case took the bag, then grabbed the pencil and used it to open the bag. He poked the contents and then took a deep whiff. "The rag looks like one from the cafeteria, but it's soaked in melted butter. Real butter. The cafeteria uses a margarine spray.

Good job, but not great. Whoever did this takes no pride in the expert forge."

Hack typed nonsense and deleted it. "Not everyone's a snob about it like you."

I looked at the burned rag. "Huh." So Case wasn't my forger. Who was? And who could have convinced twenty people that they'd seen me run to the alarm over a cafeteria grease fire? Who had that much pull with both students and teachers?

Could it be . . .

No, that was insane. She would let her grandmother go to jail before she'd break the rules. And she'd *never* forge evidence.

Maybe she did it to protect Tate. Yeah, that made sense. If I'd turned around at the last minute and denied everything, Tate would have been tried and found guilty of a crime she didn't commit. That would have offended the detective's sensitive sense of justice. Maybe she saw it as justice to fake evidence to protect an innocent, just like it was okay, by her, to lie to get into Mark's room. Or to go through my stuff during track practice.

But then, where had those twenty people who backed up my innocence come from? Why protect me, too? No ride on a grappling-hook rope was *that* much fun. At least, I didn't think so. It couldn't be her.

Case was the only forger I knew. It made more sense that Case was refusing to own up to what he saw as a substandard forge job. Yeah, that had to be it. Right?

"We saw McDuff and Natalie escorting the guy I suspect was the locker thief," Hack said. "Who would have guessed that guy Mark was behind the crime wave?"

"Who cares? I'm just glad that Tate is off the hook for the alarm," I said.

"Oh, good," Case said. "I wonder if she's free on Friday."

"I think she has soccer practice then," Hack told him.

"No worries. I'll figure something out. So this is all over?" Case asked me.

"Yeah, finally," I said. "The bad guy's caught, and everyone's getting their stuff back, though I'm not going to get any glory for retrieving it."

"Oh, don't worry. We'll make sure everyone knows what you did," Case said. "Can't have people thinking you were the locker thief."

"So I assume that means you want to hear the play-by-play."

Hack shut off the computer so fast I thought the power had gone out. "Of course!"

"SHHH!" Ms. Gimbel had come back.

"Later," I whispered. "At lunch. That will give me

some time to figure out what could possibly combine forgery and computers."

"You'll never guess it," Hack said. He looked up. "We'd better get to class. Or, at least, I should. Ms. Gimbel's giving me a weird look."

Case and I looked up. Ms. Gimbel was glaring at Hack in a way that meant she recognized him and was about to remind him, firmly, what the school's rules were regarding computer use, and then hover over him while he finished his work.

Hack stood up. "No need to attract attention now that everything's back to normal. I'll see you in homeroom." He hurried out of the library.

Case extended an Eagles-gloved hand. "Everything's back to normal, right?"

"Everything," I said, grabbing his hand. "Well, I think so. I promise."

Case nodded. "I'm glad you're still on the straight and narrow."

I snorted. "As straight and narrow as I ever can be. So, can you give me any clues about Hack's new scheme?"

"With any luck I'll talk him out of it before lunch. He wants to use the computers *here*. Can you imagine? Right under the snitch's nose. He's lost his mind."

"Yep." I had to be careful and make sure every part of

Becca's involvement in the key job was edited out when I told my story to Case and Hack. They wouldn't understand. I wasn't sure *I* did.

When Case and I left the library, I saw her. Becca was leaning against the office doors, listening in on Mark's judgment. But her eyes followed me. I saluted her, and she tried to kill me with her eyes. I saw her hand touch the camera in her pocket.

I spotted Tate in the hall, glowing with happiness. I felt guilty for the bad weekend she must have had, but at least everything had worked out. She waved as I passed, and I waved back.

Somehow the rumor that the locker thief had been caught had spread, and homeroom buzzed with happy clients. They didn't know it was me who'd stopped the thief, but they would soon. Probably before lunch, if I knew my friends. Good thing, too: I wouldn't get very many clients if everyone thought I was dirty, and the school still needed my unique brand of skills.

For example, down the row from me a girl was panicking because she'd left her geology project on the school bus, and a boy was totally engrossed in a new game. I gave him until the end of first period before the game got confiscated.

I grinned. Becca hated me, I was the leader in light

fingers at Scottsville, and students needed my services. My life was back to normal.

Or as normal as life can be for Jeremy Wilderson, retrieval specialist.

ACKNOWLEDGMENTS

This book would never have come to be without the help and efforts of so many people to whom I owe so much. Lauren E. Abramo, for being a top-notch agent. Thank you for helping me improve as a writer and for guiding me through the process of publication. I couldn't have done this without you.

Amy Cloud, for being the best editor I could ask for. Thank you for seeing the potential in my story and guiding me to find it as well.

Karen Sherman, for her careful copyediting that caught the problems I'd missed and put the final polish on the book.

Matt David, for the excellent cover illustration. You really brought my characters and story to life. Also, thanks to Karin Paprocki for the fun and dynamic cover design.

Chris Crowe, because if it wasn't for his mentoring

ACKNOWLEDGMENTS

and support, this book would never have become more than the "fun hobby story" I thought it was. Thank you for encouraging me to try something new and telling me that this story was worth writing. Thanks also go out to my classmates in his workshop for your excellent ideas and critiques. You know who you are.

My gratitude also to my family for believing in me. Thank you, Mom and Dad, for reading my writing and encouraging me, from when I was a child scribbling my first stories in crayon, to pursue my dreams. Thanks also to my sister Grace for being a patient sister and a fantastic reader, and to David, Chrisanne, Brian, Nicole, and other family members and friends who supported me and listened as I talked through story ideas with them.

READ ON

FOR A SNEAK PEEK AT THE SECOND BOOK OF JEREMY WILDERSON'S ADVENTURES!

I had no idea trouble was brewing until Case busted through my back door at sunset one Thursday during summer vacation.

Hey, don't think that because I didn't have my thumb pressed to the pulse of Scottsville's criminal activity, I'd been slacking at my job. I'm not a crime lord, and I'm not a detective like Becca Mills. My job starts *after* the crime has been committed, when the victim comes to me with a sob story and a slice of chocolate cake.

But I had tried to pay a little more attention that summer. If I'd been more attentive during the school year, I'd have known which thieves were active and that Mark was a dirty criminal psychopath who definitely did not need my help.

My contacts, like Cricket and Tomboy Tate, had gone on vacation or to camp, but the silence on the underground wasn't too odd. Summers are generally pretty chill, work-wise, for me, so on the day that all this began, I had biked, swam, and played video games with Case and Hack. Then Case went off to meet Elena Harmon at Comet Cream, which is an ice cream parlor that he frequents because it's a good place to find clients from all over town. I avoid it because Becca knows this fact.

(A note about Comet Cream: it's a small ice-cream place attached to Space Station Alpha, one of those mega-entertainment businesses that has mini golf, laser tag, and an arcade where, if you play well and earn lots of tickets, you can maybe get a key chain. Ice cream is cheap at Comet, and the whole complex is biking distance from anywhere in town. Thus, it has become a popular hangout for anyone trying to escape parents for a few hours during the summer. I went once with my family, but I prefer the games to the ice cream. Becca doesn't bother me in the arcade.)

Fast forward to an hour later, when Case burst into my house without knocking, his eyes wild.

"Dude," I said. I had been sitting near the back door, waiting for work if it came and killing time by doing summer reading (*To Kill a Mockingbird*), so I was there to greet him. "Next time, don't hold back. Just kick the door off its hinges."

"We have a problem," he said.

"Yes," a voice said. "A devious kid wearing Eagles gloves and a shifty look just infiltrated our house by the back door." My older brother Rick had made an appearance, coming in from the kitchen with a can of root beer. "Yet another illicit exchange for our Dr. Evil, and I appear to have stepped right into the middle. Oh, my, what am I to do?"

"How about you shut up and go away?" I said as Case picked at the Philadelphia Eagles logo on the back of one of his fingerless gloves. "Do your homework or read some college pamphlets."

"I'll read the pamphlets tomorrow. And summer work is better done in the heat of desperation during the last week of August," Rick said. "Preferably in the spare time between scrimmages."

Oh, right. Football camp. Like he hadn't mentioned that six times a day all summer.

"The question is," Rick said, "should I tell Mom about this little get-together now, or should I hold out for a better offer from Dr. Evil? My integrity is strong, but it can be bought." He grinned at me. "For the right price."

Case glanced from Rick to me, breathing hard. He thought Rick was serious. But I know my bonehead brother better. He knew nothing, and therefore his threat was as empty as the top half of a bag of chips.

I pointed a thumb at the stairs. "Come on, Case. Let's talk in my room. Rick's not allowed to bother me there." I glared at my brother.

"Wouldn't dream of walking into your evil lair. I'd probably step on your fluffy cat's tail and ruin the joy of any diabolic stroking. I'd hate to put my baby brother out like that."

"Oh, you got me a fluffy cat? You shouldn't have. No, really, you shouldn't have. I'm a dog person."

Rick laughed. "Joke now, if you want. But if I see blood coming from under your door or smoke from above, I'm calling the authorities."

"That was one time!" I called as I hurried Case away.

In case you were wondering, it was smoke. Case, Hack, and I were experimenting with invisible inks. Most of them are made visible with heat. We had a little accident.

"Okay," I said once I'd closed the door. "What's the urgency? You look like someone stole your art supplies."

"Not mine," Case said. "But someone *did* steal brushes and paint, and it's bad. It's so bad. I'm sorry, I told them everything. They know *everything*." He sat down on my bed, his dark skin paler than usual.